He leaned back and let the blade lull him half asleep.

Only half, though.

He could see through lowered eyelids when someone tall and burly came in.

"Long!" he blurted.

Longarm's eyes snapped open. Obviously, this fellow recognized him, but Longarm had no idea in hell who the man was.

"Who're you?"

The man didn't answer, staring intently at Longarm. And then, with a quickly spreading smile, he glanced at the gunbelt that was hanging on the coat tree.

He stepped over to place himself between Longarm and the coat tree where Longarm's Colt was hung, then reached into his coat and pulled out a short-barreled revolver.

"I am gonna kill you . . . so close your eyes and start prayin'."

# DON'T MISS THESE
## ALL-ACTION WESTERN SERIES
## FROM THE BERKLEY PUBLISHING GROUP

**THE GUNSMITH by J. R. Roberts**
Clint Adams was a legend among lawmen, outlaws, and ladies. They called him . . . the Gunsmith.

**LONGARM by Tabor Evans**
The popular long-running series about Deputy U.S. Marshal Long—his life, his loves, his fight for justice.

**SLOCUM by Jake Logan**
Today's longest-running action Western. John Slocum rides a deadly trail of hot blood and cold steel.

**BUSHWHACKERS by B. J. Lanagan**
An action-packed series by the creators of Longarm! The rousing adventures of the most brutal gang of cutthroats ever assembled—Quantrill's Raiders.

**DIAMONDBACK by Guy Brewer**
Dex Yancey is Diamondback, a Southern gentleman turned con man when his brother cheats him out of the family fortune. Ladies love him. Gamblers hate him. But nobody pulls one over on Dex . . .

**WILDGUN by Jack Hanson**
The blazing adventures of mountain man Will Barlow—from the creators of Longarm!

**TEXAS TRACKER by Tom Calhoun**
Meet J.T. Law: the most relentless—and dangerous—man-hunter in all Texas. Where sheriffs and posses fail, he's the best man to bring in the most vicious outlaws—for a price.

TABOR EVANS

# LONGARM

## AND THE COLORADO MANHUNT

JOVE BOOKS, NEW YORK

**THE BERKLEY PUBLISHING GROUP**
**Published by the Penguin Group**
**Penguin Group (USA) Inc.**
**375 Hudson Street, New York, New York 10014, USA**
Penguin Group (Canada), 90 Eglinton Avenue East, Suite 700, Toronto, Ontario M4P 2Y3, Canada
(a division of Pearson Penguin Canada Inc.)
Penguin Books Ltd., 80 Strand, London WC2R 0RL, England
Penguin Group Ireland, 25 St. Stephen's Green, Dublin 2, Ireland (a division of Penguin Books Ltd.)
Penguin Group (Australia), 250 Camberwell Road, Camberwell, Victoria 3124, Australia
(a division of Pearson Australia Group Pty. Ltd.)
Penguin Books India Pvt. Ltd., 11 Community Centre, Panchsheel Park, New Delhi—110 017, India
Penguin Group (NZ), 67 Apollo Drive, Rosedale, North Shore 0632, New Zealand
(a division of Pearson New Zealand Ltd.)
Penguin Books (South Africa) (Pty.) Ltd., 24 Sturdee Avenue, Rosebank, Johannesburg 2196,
South Africa

Penguin Books Ltd., Registered Offices: 80 Strand, London WC2R 0RL, England

This is a work of fiction. Names, characters, places, and incidents either are the product of the author's imagination or are used fictitiously, and any resemblance to actual persons, living or dead, business establishments, events, or locales is entirely coincidental.

LONGARM AND THE COLORADO MANHUNT

A Jove Book / published by arrangement with the author

PRINTING HISTORY
Jove edition / December 2007

Copyright © 2007 by The Berkley Publishing Group.
Cover illustration by Miro Sinovcic.

ISBN: 978-0-515-14386-7

JOVE®
Jove Books are published by The Berkley Publishing Group,
a division of Penguin Group (USA) Inc.,
375 Hudson Street, New York, New York 10014.
JOVE is a registered trademark of Penguin Group (USA) Inc.
The "J" design is a trademark belonging to Penguin Group (USA) Inc.

PRINTED IN THE UNITED STATES OF AMERICA

10  9  8  7  6  5  4  3  2  1

# Chapter 1

"Are you gonna draw or ain't you?"

Longarm took a deep drag on his cheroot and exhaled a series of four perfect smoke rings while he stared at the other man, jaw firm and eyes steely.

"Well?" the other demanded.

"Don't press me, dammit."

"Draw or back water, it don't make no difference to me."

"Why're you in such a hurry? You got t' take a piss or something?"

"Shit or get off the pot, Longarm."

"Yeah, hurry it up, will you," one of the other gents put in.

With a scowl and a sigh, Longarm tossed his cards down. Queen high to nothing wasn't worth staying in the pot. Dammit! His luck was at low ebb this evening, and the rest of the fellows knew it. He hadn't even been able to make a bluff hold up since he sat down. This definitely was not his night.

Longarm leaned back in his chair and eyed the curtains drawn across the stage at the head of the room. There was a new revue scheduled for the late show, and he wanted to get a look at the girls in the chorus. Otherwise, he would have called it a night before now.

He flexed his fingers and yawned, then winced when Jerry Ashe took the pot with a pair of nines. Not that he had anything better, but . . . shit! He pushed his chair back from the table and stood.

"Are you calling it a night, Longarm?"

"No, hold the seat for me. I just want t' stretch my legs an' move around a little. I'll be back."

"All right, but don't be long. We appreciate all the money you've been contributing. We'd miss it if you leave."

"Smart-ass." Longarm extinguished the stub of his cheroot in a pewter ashtray and hitched the lapels of his jacket.

Custis Long, deputy United States marshal, was well over six feet in height. He was lean, with a horseman's powerful legs and narrow waist. His shoulders were broad, as was his sweeping handlebar mustache. He had deeply tanned features and sun-wrinkles at the corners of his eyes. Longarm did not consider himself to be a handsome man or a particularly imposing one; that was a view that was disputed by a good many ladies of his acquaintance.

Standing there in Donatello's Show Palace, he was a study in brown. Dark brown hair, golden brown eyes, flat-crowned brown Stetson, brown tweed coat, light brown calfskin vest, and brown corduroy trousers stuffed into jet-black stovepipe boots.

He carried a double-action .45 Colt in a black leather cross-draw rig, the grips of the big revolver riding just to the left of his belt buckle and canted at an angle for the quickest possible draw. Not so obvious was a .41 derringer that was carried out of sight at the fob end of his watch chain in a vest pocket. Both were unfortunately much used, a necessity arising from his law enforcement duties.

The "Long Arm of the Law" arched his back to ease tight muscles and wandered through the crowded show palace floor. He nodded greetings to several acquaintances in the crowd and wound up, not surprisingly, at the thirty-foot-long polished walnut bar.

"What will it be, Longarm?"

"Rye whiskey, Don." He leaned his elbows on the bar and propped one foot on the brass rail.

"I thought you were drinking beer tonight," the bartender noted.

"I was, but there's no use keeping a clear head if I'm just gonna lose anyway," Longarm said with a grin.

"One rye, coming up."

While Longarm was watching Don's show-off moves to pour the glass of Longarm's favored Maryland distilled rye—one of the many reasons he liked Donatello's—someone moved in close to his left side. A glance in that direction showed a wiry young man in a very badly fitting blue coat and blue conductor's cap with a star pinned over a Great Western Rail Road insignia that had been embroidered there.

" 'Lo, Ralph. Care for a drink? My treat."

The young city constable shook his head. "Thanks, but I'm on duty."

"At this hour?"

"The chief asked us to work over tonight."

"This ain't usual."

"No, but he is one pissed-off fellow."

"What happened?" Longarm asked, taking his elbows off the bar and turning to face Ralph. "Something up?"

"I'll say something is up. Do you know Joe Templeton? Cuts hair in George Hauser's shop over on Grant?"

"Of course. Joe has cut my hair many a time," Longarm said.

"Joe was killed late this afternoon. Murdered."

"That don't make any sense. Everybody gets along with Joe."

"Except this time. They haven't got all the details yet, but apparently Joe was taking the day's receipts to the bank. Doing a favor for George; it wasn't something he was required to do, but I guess he had to walk that way anyhow so pretty often he would carry the receipts and make the deposit."

3

Longarm grunted. "The man was always willing to do a favor. An' for most everybody, not just for friends. He was like that."

"Well, somebody must have been expecting him, or maybe just saw the bag of money and decided on the spur of the moment to snatch it. Either way, Joe tried to hang onto the bag when the son of a bitch grabbed it. Joe wrestled him for it, so the guy took out a pistol and shot Joe in the face."

"Shit!" Longarm mumbled.

"They say Joe is still alive. Technically, I mean. He's breathing, but he has a bullet in his brain. The doctors say he won't likely wake up, though he could hang on like this for a little while."

"Damn, but I hate t' hear that," Longarm told the city constable.

"There's a lot of folks in this town that are going to hate getting that news. Joe was . . . is, I suppose I should say . . . a popular fellow."

"How's his wife taking it?"

Joe Templeton's favorite topic of conversation when he had an audience captive in his barber's chair was his family. Longarm had never met her, but he felt like he knew her well. Her name was Kate. She was originally from Ohio. She had a cat named Oscar, still was named Oscar even though Oscar had surprised the Templetons by delivering a litter of kittens last year. And Joe had a little dog that he doted on. It took Longarm a moment to remember the dog's name. Snipper. He was said—by Joe, of course—to be the smartest dog in Colorado, maybe in the whole of the United States.

Yeah, Longarm felt like he knew the Templetons, all right. Damn fine people, the sort others called the salt of the earth.

Now Joe lay dying with a bullet in his brain. And for what? A lousy bag of quarters.

There were times, Longarm thought, when the human race seemed like a collection of assholes.

He took his rye and went back to the table, but instead of sitting down to some poker he said, "I'm out, boys. Sorry."

He tossed the rye down and walked out into the night.

# Chapter 2

"Seems funny t' be talking about the laying out an' funeral arrangements when the man is still alive," Longarm mused.

"It certainly would," United States Marshal William Vail agreed with a grunt. Billy Vail, Deputy Custis Long, and the marshal's chief clerk, Henry, were gathered in Billy's office the next afternoon for an after-work tipple and cigar. It was Friday and whenever possible the three men, who had worked side by side for some years now, liked to end their week jawing about the week just used up and the week next to come. The subject of Joe Templeton had been one of the first things to come up in conversation.

"You didn't know him, Boss?" Longarm asked.

Billy Vail shook his head and with a rather rueful expression, ran a hand over his pink, gleaming, and utterly hairless scalp. "This aside," he said, "I generally shave myself."

"Joe had a nice touch with the razor," Henry said. "Besides, he was such a likable fellow. Is there any way we could look into his murder? Sort of help the Denver boys out on this one?"

The marshal shook his head again. "You both know better

7

than that. We have our own work to do. The Denver police are perfectly capable of finding a strong-arm artist."

"Or not," Longarm muttered into the glass of bourbon that Billy insisted on buying even though he knew it was tried-and-true Maryland rye that Longarm preferred.

"What? Speak up, man. You aren't on a witness stand here. No one is writing your comments down."

"What I meant t' imply . . . an' you know it . . . is that the Denver police, some of 'em anyhow, could fuck up most anything they put their minds to. Without hardly tryin'."

"Be that as it may, finding this thug is not our business. I know of no federal crime that has been committed, and we've not been asked to lend assistance. Barring that"— Billy spread his hands, palm upward—"we can do no more than wish them well. Which I am certain we all do, of course."

"Shit," Longarm grumbled.

"For once I agree with him," Henry said, nodding in Longarm's direction. "I'd like to find the man who shot Joe too."

"As would we all," Billy said. "Now about our schedule for next week. . . ."

Hauser's barbershop did not open for business on Saturday despite that normally being the most profitable day for trade. During the week, a man might stop in for a quick shave, but on the weekend he had time for a haircut too.

Longarm had expected Hauser's to be closed. He had not expected that every business in a two-block area was also closed so the shop owners could hold a vigil over the dying man.

He only learned that much courtesy of a freckle-faced paperboy who was struggling to earn a few pennies on the street corner near the barbershop.

Longarm bought a copy of the *Rocky Mountain News* from the kid and gave him a tip in return for the information.

"Look, if you can't sell your papers on this corner, why don't you go down the street a ways, get away from all these businesses that're shut down?"

"Mister, you don't know shit about the newspaper business, do ya. This corner belongs to me, see. That corner belongs to Teddy Wade, and he'd beat my ass if I tried to horn in on him."

"This Teddy guy pretty big, is he?"

"Naw."

"Then how would he whip you?"

"Him and half the other guys that sell papers on this end of town. They'd help him if I tried to move in on his corner, same as they'd help me if he tried to come here with his papers. No, sir, until Mr. Joe goes under, I won't be selling much, I can tell you. Would you like to buy another copy, mister?"

"I just bought a copy. What would I want another one for?"

"For your wife so's she can look at the ads maybe?"

Longarm laughed. "You're a helluva salesman, kid."

"So do you want that extra copy?"

"No, but here's another nickel tip."

The boy scowled and backed away. "No, thanks, mister. I don't take charity."

"Then let me buy another copy of your paper." Longarm smiled. "For my wife so she can read the advertisements."

"All right then."

"One more thing you can do for me," Longarm said.

"Yes, sir?"

"D'you know where the Templetons live? I'd like to stop by an' see if he's died yet an' where the services will be held."

"Sure, I can tell you, mister. You go down here an' cross over Cherry Creek, then turn right and . . ."

# Chapter 3

Joe Templeton died on Sunday, a fact that he might very well have appreciated. And for that matter, quite possibly did. The funeral service and the burying were held on Tuesday afternoon. Billy Vail gave Longarm, Henry, and Dutch, another of Billy's deputies, the afternoon off so they could attend the services.

"Y'know," Longarm said as they walked from the office down to the Episcopal church where the services were being held, "I think every barbershop in the city is closed t'day."

"Not just the barbers," Henry said. "A number of businesses are closing early too."

"But no saloons, t'ank gudniss," Dutch said with a grin.

"Thank goodness," Longarm agreed.

At the church, there was barely enough room for the three of them to squeeze inside. Joe Templeton had been a remarkably popular man. The eulogy delivered by the preacher was overshadowed by the news that raced by whispered word of mouth through the mourners: The killer had been captured.

Denver police, they said, identified the murderer as Karl Edward Hix, a small-time hoodlum and petty thief known for running crooked shell games and rolling drunks in dark

11

alleys. He was captured by a squad of Denver police after a bank teller turned him in when Hix tried to exchange a bag of quarters for currency. The killer surrendered meekly when the police confronted him.

"You know this man, Longarm?" Dutch asked, forgetting to keep his booming voice down to a whisper.

"Shh! Yeah, I know the sonuv . . ." Longarm glanced up at the soaring arches and stained glass that sheltered them. "Yeah, I know who he is. Seen him on the street. Never had reason t' pay no real attention to him, though."

"Same as me," Dutch said. Loudly.

"Will you two please shut up," Henry hissed.

"Sorry," Longarm whispered.

The service concluded with an announcement about where the interment would be and that the family would be at home to receive sympathy calls that evening.

"You go to cemetery?" Dutch asked.

Longarm shook his head. "No, but I'll stop by the house this evenin'. What about you, Henry?"

"I have work to do. I really shouldn't have taken the time to come over here, but Joe was such a good fellow. I'm glad we came."

"*Ja.* Me too," Dutch said as they walked back to the office.

The street was filled with the hundreds who had been at the funeral service. Very few seemed to be making the ride out to the cemetery with the coffin and the pallbearers.

That evening, when the last writ was served and the last of his paperwork—damn, but he did hate paperwork—was turned in, Longarm stopped at one of the many small cafés in the downtown area. This one was run by a fat, forever-laughing Italian woman who made a macaroni dish that Longarm loved. He drew the line at accepting the red, fruity wine she always tried to give him, though, and insisted on having a pail of beer brought in to drink with his meal instead.

•  •  •

After supper, he walked on to the Widow Templeton's house, where women were scurrying inside, carrying bowls and platters and trays of food, while the men who had already been inside gathered in the tiny front yard to smoke and reminisce about what a good fellow Joe had been.

Longarm mounted the steps and took his hat off, then stepped into the stifling hot parlor to join the line of folks who came to express their sympathies. He approached the lady, who was dressed all in black and seated beside a young man who Longarm assumed was someone from the church or perhaps a relative of some sort.

"Miz Templeton. I just . . ." He really did not know what to say. "I'm awful sorry for your loss."

"Thank you, sir. Thank you very much."

Longarm glanced at the young fellow seated next to her. He nodded.

"This is our son," Kate Templeton said. Not that Longarm had any intention of asking. "This is Joe Junior."

"Mother. Please don't."

"Joe Junior," his mother said, as if insisting upon it.

It seemed strange that Joe had never mentioned having a son. Whatever was going on here, Longarm did not know what it was and did not want to. He very quickly and very lightly shook Joe Templeton Jr.'s hand and hurried back outside, passing up the mountains of fried chicken and cornbread, passing as well the knots of men who were standing around smoking and gossiping.

Longarm figured his respects for a very nice but only casually known fellow had been properly paid and the murderer was behind bars. That, he figured, was the end of it. He would not be having anything more to do with Joe Templeton's killing.

He was wrong. Almost dead wrong.

# Chapter 4

Longarm woke slowly. His sleep had been deep, the result of sheer exhaustion. Now he felt disoriented and groggy, his mind fogged by the power of sleep.

He felt . . . like he was immersed in warm water. Like he was floating. Warm. But aroused.

And he had a strong desire to take a piss even though his bladder did not feel all that full. The wet warmth overcame a lifelong reluctance to soil the bed, and he felt the escape of a trickle of urine. Just a little. Then a little more.

He heard a low mumble and felt the bed move and the sheet pull away. A moment later, the red-haired girl from the chorus line—what the hell was her name anyway . . . Mary, that was it, maybe—sat up at his side. She was grinning.

"That woke you up, hey!"

"What the . . . oh, shit."

"No, it's all right. It was my own fault for waking you up all wet like that."

"But I . . . you know."

"Really, Custis, I'm telling you, it didn't taste all that bad. A little salty. Tangy, sort of. Of course pee doesn't taste as good as cum. I love the taste of cum. Can't get enough of

15

it. But pee isn't bad as a substitute. Do you want to get rid of the rest of your morning load? I'll drink it if you want."

"Uh, no. Thank you, but no. What was that you were saying about drinking cum, though?"

The girl's grin got wider. "Can I have a little taste of yours?"

"I did have that in mind, dear." Longarm was not normally given to the use of terms of endearment with casual lady friends. But he was not quite sure about this one's correct name, and it would be damn well insulting—to say nothing of the embarrassment—if he got her name wrong while she was in the process of sucking his cock.

"Then why don't you lie back and let Miss Margaret do for you."

Margaret! It wasn't Mary, dammit. Margaret. At least it began with an M. He'd gotten that much right.

Margaret pushed her mass of flowing auburn hair out of the way, either so it would not interfere or so he could more easily watch his cock slide in and out of her pretty mouth, and bent to him.

Longarm was already fully erect by then. Margaret was not a girl who knew how to overcome the gag reflex and take a dick deep into her throat. He'd learned that the evening before. But she was a sweet and willing little cocksucker—little! she was almost as tall as he—and she did seem to enjoy it, more actually than normal fucking. But then a girl could not get pregnant from a dick in her mouth. Perhaps that was what made the difference.

Now she licked and sucked happily away, swirling the head of his cock around and around with her tongue, dipping her head now and then to lick his balls and work her way back up the length of his glistening shaft.

"That feels . . . damn good."

It did too. Very good. And she had been kind enough to refrain from asking for a kiss after he inadvertently pissed in her mouth. Thoughtful of her.

She cupped his balls in one hand and squeezed his shaft with the other and sucked so hard he thought she might bring his toenails squirting out of the blind snake.

What she did very soon get was a gasp and a lunge of Longarm's hips as the sweet, hot sensations gathered in his balls and burst out.

A load of cum spat into Margaret's mouth without warning.

The pretty girl moaned and squeezed him tighter while she continued to suck. He could feel her throat constrict over and over as she swallowed his seed, staying there and sucking the last possible drops out of his body. When she finished—and it took a while before she was satisfied that she had it all—Margaret sat up and rocked back onto her knees, a cheerful smile on her face.

"Now I'm all confused," she said. "I can't decide which tastes better, dear, your pee or your cum. I like them both. I really do."

"Then maybe you can make a proper test o' them later," Longarm suggested.

"I'd like that, dear."

"But right now, little darlin', it's comin' morning, and I got t' go t' the office. See what the boss has for me today."

Margaret hopped lightly out of bed and reached for his smallclothes, obviously expecting to help him dress. Not that he really minded. If a man was going to have a valet, it might as well be a tall, naked, red-haired Valkyrie with long legs and big tits.

Margaret went so far as to hold his coat for him while Longarm buckled his gunbelt in place. Then she hugged him and sighed happily.

"I won't ask you to kiss me good-bye. You understand why, I think. But I'll have cleaned my teeth before you see me again. So . . . tonight maybe? Can I see you again?"

"I'd like that," Longarm said. "I surely would." He picked up his Stetson and settled it comfortably in place, then smiled and touched the brim. He turned away toward the door of her room, then on an impulse turned back and took the lass into his arms.

Her mouth was soft and eager and he did not taste anything unpleasant there.

"Later," he said.

He hailed a hansom outside the showgirls' hotel and had it drop him at a café. After breakfast—huge; he was positively famished after a night spent in the middle of the eager and athletic Miss Margaret—he walked the rest of the way to the Federal Building.

"Mornin', Henry," Longarm said as he hung his hat on the clothes tree in the corner. "Is the boss in yet?" The question was a joke. Billy Vail was *always* in. Or it seemed like it anyway. Longarm could almost have sworn that Billy slept in his office.

"I don't know what he has for you today, so take a seat and wait a bit. He'll get to you when he's ready."

"Is that today's newspaper I see over there?" Longarm asked.

Henry reached for the folded copy of the *Rocky Mountain News* and handed it to Longarm. "Today's interesting news isn't in there," Henry said.

"What's that?"

"Do you remember that fellow, uh, Karl Hix?"

"Sure. Hix is the sonuvabitch that shot Joe Templeton. Denver cops got him two days ago. I figure he'll never see anything but gray stone an' steel bars for the rest o' his days. An' good riddance."

"Wrong," Henry said.

"Par'n me?"

"City Judge Delmar Watrous dismissed the charges against him and turned Hix loose already."

"What!"

"Unbelievable, isn't it," Henry said.

"That son of a fucking bitch," Longarm grumbled.

18

"Which one are you talking about, Hix or Watrous?"

"Either o' the bastards. Both o' them. Shit. Henry, you just ruined my whole damn day."

"Hix may be a son of a bitch," Henry said, "but not Judge Watrous. Judges never make mistakes. Don't believe me? Ask Judge Watrous."

"I swear, I'm half-tempted t' do exactly that, Henry. Jesus!"

"You could ask Jesus too, I suppose. Somehow, I don't think you would get the same answer." Henry sighed and shook his head. "Watrous is a dyed-in-the-wool son of a bitch."

Longarm only growled and stomped across the room to take a seat on one of the chairs against the wall opposite Henry's broad desk. He snapped the newspaper open, but the articles he read did not penetrate his thoughts any further than his eyeballs. He was just too damned angry to have any idea what he was reading.

That cocksucking prick!

And again, he himself was not sure which he meant by that. It seemed to apply equally to Karl Hix and to Delmar Watrous.

# Chapter 5

Longarm had a lunch of crackers, beer, and hot pickled sausages. The sausages sometimes came back on him, but he did dearly love the things.

He stood hunkered over the bar, brooding over the frequent injustices of the justice system and wearing a scowl that prompted others to give him a wide berth.

"Another beer, Longarm?"

"Yeah. Why the hell not."

The gent in the dirty apron picked up Longarm's mug—no sense having to wash another one—and shoved it under the tap. "Any exciting robberies or whatever lately?" Longarm asked.

"Naw, nothing special. Couple stagecoach holdups where mail got tooken, that's all."

"Routine," Longarm said.

"That sounds exciting enough for my taste," the bartender said as he whisked the top suds off the newly filled mug, added a smidgen more beer, and set the overflowing mug in front of Longarm.

"How about that guy that murdered Joe Templeton? Are you federal boys going after him?"

Longarm shook his head. "That's a local matter. Besides, the judge has already turned Hix loose. You know him, don't you?"

"Sure I do, but just as a customer. The cops are looking for him again, though."

"How come?"

"What I heard is that they found a witness. Hix was released last night; then this morning, someone came forward and admitted to seeing him pull off the robbery."

"Shit!" Longarm snorted.

"It's lousy," the bartender agreed. "By now, Karl will be miles away and running fast. Not that I suppose he really needs to worry about being caught again. The only people who care are here in Denver. He can change his name and never have to look over his shoulder again."

"Thank you, Judge Asshole Watrous," Longarm complained.

After a few minutes, as he was reaching the end of the mug of beer, he straightened his posture and a look of deep concentration melted into his usually mild expression.

"Bob," he called to the bartender.

The man set his towel aside, glanced along the length of the bar to make sure he was not missing any trade, then wandered over to Longarm's end of the counter. "Another beer, Longarm?"

"No, I'm done. But listen, a minute ago you mentioned something about Karl Hix. An' you said something about the mail being took, isn't that right?"

"Well, what I actually did was to ask . . ."

"Hold it." Longarm held his palm up and stepped back away from the bar. "Don't say no more."

The bartender gave him a questioning look. "If you say so."

Longarm grinned, the first such expression he had shown

since early morning. "Yeah. I do. Thanks, Bob. Thanks a lot. I'll explain t' you later."

"Sure. Whatever you say."

Longarm walked back to the Federal Building with a light and eager stride.

# Chapter 6

"Billy, there's a case I want t' be assigned to," Longarm said.

U.S. Marshal William Vail leaned back in his swivel chair, the springs underneath it protesting as he did so. Sunlight coming in from the window behind him gleamed off Billy's bald dome. Billy's head was so shiny that Longarm sometimes suspected the boss polished it. Lanolin maybe? "That's a new wrinkle," Billy said, "you stepping up and asking for work. What is this about? Have you found some new floozy who makes you want to stay close to the city?"

"This is somethin' that'd make me leave the city, Boss. It ain't no holiday I'm lookin' for. But I admit straight out that I got a personal interest in this one."

"Now you have my interest piqued. Tell me what it is, please."

"Robbery o' the mails, Billy. I overheard somethin' when I was havin' lunch."

"Tell me about it."

"What I heard, Boss, an' it wasn't too clear, mind you, what I heard was somethin' about robbing the mails an' practically in the same breath talk about Karl Hix. I didn't hear everything, but what I heard was enough t' make me think that maybe, just maybe, Hix is responsible for one o' those

25

stagecoach holdups. Like t' get some coin in his pocket so's he can run. Finance his getaway, so t' speak. Like I said, I'm not for sure about it. But I'd like t' be the one t' follow it up. I'd like t' go after Hix an' bring him in to justice."

"Murder is not a federal crime," Vail said, leaning forward in his chair and giving his top deputy a long look.

"I know that, Boss. But robbery o' the mail sure as shit is. An' there was a mail pouch taken in that stagecoach holdup."

Billy leaned back again, his chair squealing in protest. He laced his fingers over his waistcoat and spun around to peer out the window for a moment. When he turned back around again, he grunted softly, then nodded. "All right. It is your tip to follow. But dammit, Custis, as you pursue this thing, if you find that someone other than Hix was the robber, I want you to drop Hix as your suspect and stay on the trail of the real robber. Do we understand each other?"

"Yes, sir," Longarm said solemnly.

Billy sat forward and put his palms flat on his desk. "I understand that Templeton was a friend of yours. I appreciate the fact. But do not forget your sworn duty."

"Yes, sir."

"You can draw expense authorization slips from Henry on your way out. Tell him I approve them. And, um, he can go ahead and sign my name to them. He might as well. He does my signature better than I do anyway."

"I didn't think . . ." Longarm stopped what he had been about to say and clamped his mouth shut.

Billy permitted a hint of a smile to tickle the corners of his mouth. "Didn't think I knew about that? Longarm. Really! I know more than you may think about what goes on around here. And I suggest you keep that in mind."

"I will, Boss. Believe me, I will." Longarm resisted an impulse to salute—God, where had that come from after all these years—turned, and marched smartly out of Billy's office.

# Chapter 7

"How will you go about finding this fellow?" Henry asked as he handed over a sheaf of vouchers that Longarm could fill out and give to stores or hotels or whatever so the government would pay them for their services.

Longarm shrugged. "The usual, I reckon. Find out where the man lived. If he had a horse. Family. Places he talked about. It's all routine stuff."

"I hope you find the son of a bitch," Henry hissed.

"You s'prise me, old friend. You don't gen'rly use words like that."

"That doesn't mean I don't know them. And in this case, I happen to think they apply. Joe Templeton was a good man. He didn't deserve what Karl Hix did to him."

"There's not many deserve that kinda treatment, Henry."

"No, but it seems like we have to deal with most of the ones who do."

Longarm folded his vouchers and tucked them into an inside pocket of his coat. "No tellin' when I'll get back, Henry."

"If you need help, I'll be glad to lend a hand," the mild-mannered clerk offered. The odd thing was that as gently as he talked and looked and acted, Henry was a sure hand with a gun and could be counted on when the lead was flying. As Longarm had had more than one occasion to find out. Henry's offer was sincere.

"I'll remember that, old friend." Longarm plucked his Stetson off the coatrack and set it onto his head at a slight angle, nodded to Henry, and headed out onto the streets of Denver.

A brisk walk of only a dozen blocks or so took him from the dignified neighborhood of the Federal Building and the United States Mint, past the State Capitol Building and his favorite watering holes, to the seamy underside of Denver where the women and the liquor were cheap and where both were plentiful. The saloons were open around the clock, and a man could buy almost anything if he had a little brass in his pocket.

Longarm had heard of one instance when a man had a rival murdered for a two-dollar bottle of whiskey and a silver dollar, the reason being that he wanted the poor bastard's common-law wife.

Bless these lowlifes' hearts, Longarm mused as he entered the district. If it weren't for the likes of them, he would not have a job. And he was about half serious about it.

He stepped around a pile of garbage that was spilling out of the mouth of an alley onto the sidewalk, and paused outside a place that had no name he'd ever heard but that was known locally as The Rat House. With good reason.

"Shee-it," Longarm mumbled to himself as he took a moment to adjust the angle of his hat and to make sure his Colt lay free in the leather, "the things I hafta do for the lady that holds up the scales o' justice." He pushed in through the curtain of fly beads that hung in the doorway, the wooden beads clattering to announce the arrival of a customer.

As soon as he stepped in, he was inundated with the sour stink of beer and puke and sawdust that should have been replaced years ago. The place smelled of sweat and

28

cigar smoke, and even at this hour of the morning—he did not check his watch, but figured it should be around 9:30 or so—there was a card game in progress at one table and a man passed out across another. Passed out or maybe dead. No one seemed to much care which.

The bartender was a pinch-faced one-armed man who looked like he might have last bathed when Grant was still trying to take Richmond. Half a dozen men were idling at the bar. All of them turned their heads to see who was joining them.

"Well," said a tall gent whose mustache was even bushier than Longarm's, "if it ain't the long arm of the law who's come amongst us." He turned to speak to the others at the bar. "Watch yourselfs, boys. This here is the one they call Longarm. He'd rather kill you than go to the trouble of taking you in to the jail." To Longarm, he said, "Which of us are you gunning for today, eh?"

Longarm smiled. "Good morning to you too, Sammy. It's always nice t' see you."

The man most recently known as Sammy—he had had other names in the past—hurriedly tossed down his drink, then turned and left. So did all but one of the other early morning imbibers. The one who remained was only standing upright because he had the bar to hang on to; he looked like one more drink would put him facedown on the floor.

"D'you want a beer, Long?" the barkeep grunted as Longarm stepped around an overturned cuspidor and approached the bar. The bartender was a stout, muscular fellow whose hair was receding far back from where his forehead used to end.

"No, thanks."

"You mean you come in here and chase away all my customers and then won't even buy a lousy beer?"

"Ayuh, that's what it looks like. You can make up for the loss of trade easy enough. Just throw another couple gallons of dishwater into that barrel."

"I don't water my . . ."

"Oh, shut up about that, Edgar. I don't care what you do to your beer nor t' that rotgut you sell as whiskey neither. I'm here looking for somebody an' the quicker I find out what I want t' know, the quicker I'll be outta your hair . . . what of it that you got left . . . and out that door."

"So what do you want to know?"

"Karl Hix," Longarm said. "You know the man."

"Who says I do?"

"I say it." Longarm ambled up to the bar and propped a foot on the brass rail in front of it. "He used to drink here." That was only a guess. He had no idea where Hix used to hang out.

"What if he did?"

"So you can tell me about him," Longarm said.

"He likes whiskey and he never paid more than fifty cents for a woman in his life," Edgar said.

"Cheap?"

"In spades. But if you're looking for him, you're in the wrong place, Long. What I heard is that he left town a couple days ago."

"Where'd he go?"

Edgar shook his head. "I don't know. Don't care neither. I never let him run a tab here so he doesn't owe me anything."

"Where's he live?"

"I wouldn't know that neither."

"What do you know about him then? You want to help me all you can, Edgar. You want t' do that because you're such a good citizen. An' maybe also because I got some friends on the city police force that'd be happy t' come in here an' roust you an' your customers three, four, maybe half a dozen times a night." Longarm paused and smiled. "Every night."

"I already told you . . ."

"You already told me shit. Now give me something that I can work with, Edgar, or you might find it hard t' keep up your payments to Boss Hardy. An' think what that would mean." Hardy was at the top of the heap of Denver's trash. He ran a protection racket and tended to become irritable when payments were missed.

"I told you everything I know about the son of a bitch."

"All right, Edgar. I believe you." Longarm smiled and touched the brim on his hat. As he turned to leave, he said, "We'll see if your memory has improved any after a week or so with bluecoat coppers staking out the place."

"No. Wait. I know . . ." Edgar licked his lips and looked around, but it did not really matter if anyone was observing this or not. He had to give at least a little. "I know this whore Hix favored. God knows why. Maybe she'd do him for nothing when he was broke, but I got the idea the two of them went back a way. She might know something about him. Her name is Marie. Yellow Feather Marie. She's . . ."

"I know who she is," Longarm said. "Where is Marie working these days?"

Edgar shrugged. "One of the cheap places along the row."

Longarm looked around slowly, then turned back to Edgar and raised an eyebrow.

"I mean really cheap. Try the Rainbow."

The Rainbow would be the saloon that was more formally named The End of the Rainbow. But there was no pot of gold there. Hell, there was not even a pot of spit on the premises, they being too stingy to put cuspidors down for their customers. Instead, people just spat on the floor.

"Yeah, I know the Rainbow," Longarm said.

"Look for Yellow Feather Marie there. Last I heard, that's where she was working."

"All right. But I may be back. See if there's anything

31

else you can remember about Hix in the meantime, Edgar. It could be important to you."

"Damn you, Long."

"Have a nice day, Edgar." Longarm touched the brim of his Stetson and smiled, then ambled out onto the street, the fly beads clacking and clattering behind him.

# Chapter 8

"Sorry. I don't know nobody named Yella Feather Marie."

"I heard that you do."

"Then you heard wrong, mister."

"It's deputy, not mister. Deputy United States Marshal."

"I know who you are. I know what you are. I also know my rights. You got no jurisdiction here."

"Ever hear about a charge called 'obstruction o' justice'?"

"Go fuck yourself." The bartender at the Rainbow turned away and walked to the other end of his bar.

Longarm shrugged. He palmed his .45 in one hand and his badge in the other. He triggered a bullet into the ornate lead sheathing that covered the ceiling and held the badge high for everyone to see. The Rainbow was empty in a matter of mere seconds.

"Damn you!" the barman screamed.

Longarm said, "It was your choice, but I can do it as often as I please. Want t' see it again sometime real soon?"

"Yella Feather Marie, you said?"

"That's right. Where's her crib?"

"She doesn't have a crib of her own. Can't afford to rent one. When she's working, she mostly does guys in the alley out back. I think she hires a bed from some straight girl.

Some kind of do-gooder or something like that. I'll draw you a sketch of how to find this girl. Marie calls her Itsy Bitsy. Marie should be there or at least Bitsy can tell you where she is. Here. This should get her."

"Thanks for your cooperation." Longarm touched the brim of his hat and left.

Bitsy's room was only a few blocks away. Apparently, this Itsy Bitsy had more going for her than giving twenty-five-cent blow jobs or fifty-cent fucks. She lived in a converted stable behind a rooming house, but it was an attractive conversion. There were potted flowers flanking the door and lacy curtains billowing softly at the windows, and the outside was handsomely painted and in good repair.

Longarm tapped lightly on the door. No one answered, so he rapped again, harder. And again a few minutes later. Finally, he banged loudly and kept it up until the door was unlocked and opened a crack.

"Bitsy?" He could only see half of the woman's face, but what he could see was pretty enough. She had gleaming jet hair and blue eyes. At least, her left eye was a bright and brilliant blue; he could not see the other.

"Whatever you're selling, mister, I'm not interested."

Longarm held his badge in front of her eye.

"Police?"

"Deputy United States marshal."

"What do you want with me?"

"I'm looking for Yellow Feather Marie. I understand she sleeps here."

"Sometimes."

"Like now?"

"Is Marie in trouble?"

"No. No trouble. I just need t' talk to her. She might know somethin' that'll help me with a case I'm workin' on."

"She's here. Give me a minute to wake her. She had a hard night."

"All of Marie's nights are hard, Bitsy."

34

The girl with the blue eyes sighed. "I know. Wait here."

The door was shut and he could hear the sound of a bolt being pushed closed. Still, the girl had said to wait, and there had been no animosity in her voice. He waited.

It was several long minutes later, long enough to make him wonder if Bitsy was trying to pull something on him to let Marie get away, before he heard the bolt move again. The door opened a little—beyond it he got a glimpse of a very nicely appointed and very clean little apartment—and Yellow Feather Marie stepped out.

Longarm had seen her a number of times, mostly back in the day when she was working a better class of saloon than seemed to be the case now. He was shocked when he saw her. He remembered a girl who was lively and smiling. This . . . this was a pale skeleton of a creature who looked to be only half a step away from the grave. Even powder and rouge could not disguise the diseased countenance in front of him. Longarm snatched his hat off. "Hello, Marie."

"Longarm!" She sounded pleased to see him.

He had never paid any attention before, but now he was struck by Marie's eyes. They were a bright and brilliant blue. The same blue, he thought, that he had just seen at the door.

On a hunch, he said, "Bitsy's your sister, isn't she?"

"Yeah, why?"

"Is she in the life?"

Marie shook her head. "Not Bitsy. Our daddy sold us to a fella, but Bitsy got out of it. She works for a dentist in town here. Nice man too. He . . . he don't know about when Bitsy and me was little." She blinked and paused for a moment. "You ain't gonna tell him, are you?"

"No, Marie, that isn't what I came here t' talk about. There's something you can help me with."

"Yeah. I never had no hard feelings for you, Longarm." She smiled a phony professional smile and laid her fingertips on his wrist. "Handsome gentleman like you. I'd be real pleased to do you. I'm a good lay too. Ask anybody."

"I've heard you're a fine lay, Marie," he lied, "but I'm working. I'm looking for a friend of yours. Karl Hix. Do you know where he's gone?"

"Karl is gone? Where'd he go?"

"That's what I'm hoping you can tell me, Marie. He is a friend of yours, isn't he?"

"Yeah, you could say that. He's one of my regulars." She smiled. "I don't have so many of those no more. I can't afford to lose any if I can help it. Jeez, I'm gonna hate it if I lose Karl too."

"So can you help me, Marie?"

"Let me think." She turned away, leaning on the door of her sister's tidy little carriage house like she would fall down if she did not have something to prop herself upright. After a few moments, she turned back to face Longarm.

"I don't know where he's gone, but Karl used to talk sometimes about Colorado City and Manitou. I know he liked those places awful well. I think he got into some sort of trouble down there, which is why he come up to Denver. But I think the whole time he was here, he was wishing he was back there. If it was me, I'd look for him down there."

"All right, Marie. Thank you." He put his hat back on and smiled, then started to turn away.

Marie touched him on the wrist again. "Longarm."

"Yeah, baby."

"If you . . . you know . . . if you're horny . . . I could give you a good price. Straight fuck. French. Greek. Work a threesome or a freak show. Whatever you want, honey."

The thought of putting his dick anywhere in or on this poor diseased creature made his skin crawl. God knows how many diseases she had.

"Thanks, baby. I would but I don't have time right now. I have to go find Karl."

"Maybe later then?"

"Sure. Maybe later." He resisted an impulse to slip her a few dollars. Obviously, money was not what she needed.

The truth was that it was probably years too late for what she once needed, for what her sister Bitsy got and Marie did not.

"Thanks for your help, Marie."

Colorado City, eh? Longarm was thinking about his next stop before he ever got out of Itsy Bitsy's garden.

# Chapter 9

Longarm liked Colorado City. It was not big but it was . . . friendly, one might call it. Very friendly. He never saw any statistics on the subject, but he figured there might be more whores to the acre in Colorado City than in anyplace else in the country. But then there was money in Colorado City. Money pouring in to the smelters that refined gold from all over the high country that lay just to the west. And money has a tendency to attract both whores and whiskey. Colorado City had more than its fair share of each.

Which, Longarm thought, was not an entirely bad thing.

He stepped down from the Colorado Springs-to-Manitou short-line railroad train, laden with saddle, rifle, and carpetbag, and walked to the edge of the platform, cinders crunching underfoot. There was never a porter around when you wanted one, he reflected. Nor a cab.

Not that he needed a cab at the moment. Ginny Byerlie's Tejas House was only a block and a half away. And despite the suggestions that might arise from the name, the place was a decent hotel, not a whorehouse.

He walked the short distance, mounted the steps to the porch, and let himself in to the lobby.

"Hello, Ginny. Still screwing your customers, I see," he said, nodding toward a sign posted behind the desk that stated rooms were five dollars per night or twenty-seven fifty by the week.

"How do you mean that, Longarm?"

He chuckled. It was an open secret that Ginny had made her pile first as a brighter-than-most whore somewhere in Louisiana, then as a madam in Galveston. Now she lived in Colorado City to keep an eye on her many investments in both mining and milling. She ran the Tejas House to keep herself occupied rather than to make a living.

Ginny came around from behind the front desk and gave Longarm a playful bump with her hip. "It will be the old room rate for you, handsome. Or completely free of charge if you want to sleep in my bed." She laughed at the joke she always made when he arrived, but he suspected she was more than half serious about it too.

She was, he thought, in her seventies. At least. And she looked like a stiff breeze would blow her over or a stiff dick shock her senseless. Neither was true. Ginny was a tough old bat if ever he saw one, and he wished for her sake that she could find some old codger who could still get it up and move him into that bedroom. Longarm liked Ginny Byerlie right well.

"Who are you after this time, dearie?" she asked as she spun the guest register around for him to sign and handed him a pen. Ginny always insisted that the register be signed. She did not, however, care what name a man chose to write there.

"You wouldn't know his kind, Ginny. His name is Karl Hix. Strictly a penny-ante lowlife. He's wanted for a lot of things including suspicion of robbing the U.S. mails."

"Not for murder?"

"How'd you know about that?"

"I read the newspapers, sweetheart."

"Hell, Ginny, I thought all you'd bother reading was the financial pages."

"I don't have a man, Longarm. That means I have time on my hands, enough that I can keep up with things. But there are other things I wouldn't mind having on my hands." She looked at Longarm's crotch and winked, then broke into raucous laughter when he said, "I'll have to let you know about that later, Ginny."

"I tell you what, dear. I have some eyes and ears in this town. I'll ask around about Hix and see what I can come up with. In the meantime, make yourself to home. Number six, upstairs front so you can keep an eye out on the street the way I know you like to do. I still don't want the bother of serving meals to my regular guests, but you can join me in the kitchen if you like. No charge."

"You're a sweetheart yourself, Ginny. It's just a damn shame I didn't meet you when you were a few years younger."

She smiled. "A few?"

"Whatever."

He gave the old broad a kiss on the forehead and trudged up the stairs with his things.

He did not see Ginny all that often, but it was always a pleasure when he did.

# Chapter 10

There were some decent saloons in town where a gentleman could relax in tasteful surroundings, places where the
floors were polished and the cigars of the best quality, places
where brandy was served in proper snifters or whiskey in
glasses. Karl Hix was not going to be found in any of
those.

Instead, Longarm headed for the other extreme when
it came to liquor. Colorado City also had more than its
share of those. Places where the floors were covered with
tobacco juice and sawdust, the liquor consisted of creek
water and rattlesnake venom, and it was a toss-up whether
the whores carried more diseases than they did fleas. That
was the sort of place Hix would want. And could afford.
The asshole had not gotten much of a haul in that bag of
quarters from the barbershop. No wonder he had returned
to familiar surroundings when he had to go on the run.

Longarm started at one end of the eight-block-long
saloon district, figuring to work his way up one side of the
street, cross over to the other, and make his way back
again, stopping in at each place to look for Hix.

It took no time at all to learn that Hix was known down
here. The barman at the first joint he stopped in came to the

end of the bar, towel in hand, and nodded a greeting that was more suspicious than friendly. But then, Longarm was not exactly dressed like a teamster or a milling machine operator.

"Whada ya want?"

"Information," Longarm said.

"We serve beer."

"I'm looking for a man."

"You want a man? So which are you, a queer or a cop?"

"I'm a deputy U.S. marshal, and I asked you a question."

The bartender nodded. "Sure you did. So who's the lucky sonuvabitch you's looking for?"

"Fella named Karl Hix. He used t' live here."

"Lots of folks used to live here but don't no more."

"Well, this one has come back."

"Zat so?"

"Uh-huh. So have you seen him?"

"I don't think so."

"D'you know him?"

"I don't think so."

"It occurs t' me that you don't seem t' know a whole helluva lot."

"You want a beer or don't you?"

"No, I don't want a beer," Longarm said.

Now wouldn't that be a fine idea. He could stop in and have a beer at each and every joint on the strip. That would be . . . what? Twenty? Thirty places? Thirty beers? Even watered beer like he could expect in these shitty saloons would have a man walking on his knees and puking out his guts after thirty of them. No, he did not think it would be a very good idea to start pouring down the suds in each joint.

On the other hand, it would be interesting to see Henry's response if he reported that sort of night on the town on his expense sheet. Shit, it would almost be worth getting that sick just to see Henry's face when he asked for reimbursement.

"D'you know Hix or don't you?" Longarm persisted.

"Go fuck yourself." The bartender turned away and headed toward his bank of kegs. That would also, Longarm noted, be where he was likely to store his bung starter, a device equally useful as a club to pound a skull or a beer keg closure.

Perhaps, Longarm reflected, he should reconsider his approach to the search for Karl Hix.

He left that saloon and headed on to the one next door.

# Chapter 11

The barkeep grunted low in his throat, then turned his head and spat, the gob of phlegm landing in a tub of dirty mugs waiting to be washed. Or just wiped and set back on the counter. Longarm made a mental note to avoid drinking around here. Ever again.

"I don't care if you claim to be the guy's Aunt Susie from Baltimore. I don't carry no messages. Not for nobody. I mind my own business. You'd best mind yours."

"Thanks a lot." Longarm was not sure the man even heard him. By the time Longarm spoke, the barkeep had already turned away and was reaching for a spigot to draw another beer.

"Hello, sweetheart. Care to go outside?" The whore needed to wash her face and try again. Her makeup was layered on so thick she looked like a circus clown in drag.

On the other hand, that might well have been an improvement on what was underneath all that powder and paint. "What's outside?" Longarm asked.

"Whatever you want, baby."

"You got a crib back there?"

"Sure, baby. You want a bed, I can give you one. That's ten cents extra, but I can see that wouldn't be a problem for a fine, handsome gentleman like you." She smiled, exposing several gaps where teeth had been knocked out. Someone ought to knock the rest of them out, Longarm mused. The old broad would make a fortune giving blow jobs.

"You wouldn't have some 'friends' in the alley waitin' to roll me for my poke, would you?" Longarm said.

"No, honey, I wouldn't do any such thing."

"An' I trust you too. Indeed I do." Longarm smiled too. But he had all his teeth. "Let's go."

"You haven't even asked me how much."

"That's because I already know," he said, "an' it happens t' be more than you'd think."

"Really? How rough are you going to get? You'll leave me able to still work, won't you?"

"Does it matter?"

"Well, yeah. If I'm going to be laid up for more'n a day, I expect you to cover my losses for that time. And you can't break bones. I draw the line there. Nothing busted. You understand?"

"Sure. Nothing busted."

The whore turned and covered her mouth when she yawned. The gesture looked phony and probably was a signal to someone in the place, although whether she was warning them off or telling them to try to take him he could not know.

She led the way into a trash-strewn alley, walked past the outhouse that served the businesses on this side of the block, and turned into an even narrower way. If there was going to be anyone waiting to strong-arm him, this was likely to be the spot, he guessed, but they passed without incident, the whore playing straight with him.

She took him inside a rickety crib and bolted the door behind them. "Now what is it you want, honey? Tell me that first, then we'll discuss the price for that service."

"What I want is information."

"That's all?"

He nodded.

"You a cop?"

"No." It was not a lie. Exactly. He was a federal deputy, not a police officer.

"What sort of information, dearie?"

"I'm looking for a man. I heard he can do a particular sort of work, never mind exactly what sort of job I have in mind. It would be worth an eagle for me to find him."

The old whore's eyes went wide, and he realized he'd just offered too much. She probably had not seen ten dollars, not of her own, in a long time. Hell, she probably did not earn that much in a week's time. The problem was that she was very likely thinking there was something fishy about the offer.

"Tell me his name. Maybe I know him."

If she did know Hix, and did not believe Longarm's offer, she would be more apt to warn Hix than to finger him, Longarm realized.

"Daniel Raven," he said. "I'm looking for a man name of Dan Raven." Raven was a deputy constable in Golden. For no reason in particular his was the first name that popped into mind.

"I never heard of him."

"Well, if you do, it's worth that eagle."

"I'll ask around," she lied.

"Good." He turned to leave. He hadn't even taken his hat off. The whore stopped him with a touch on his elbow.

"The room," she said. "I got to pay for it whether we fuck or not."

He gave her a quarter to cover both the room and her time, then got the hell out of there.


"I'm looking for a man."

The look of hooded suspicion he received in return was expected. So was the bartender's silence.

"I got a job of work for him t' do," Longarm added.

That brought the bartender closer to his whiskey-stained bar. He leaned forward and in a hushed voice asked, "What sort of work would that be?"

"The sort that isn't any o' your nevermind," Longarm told him, "an' I already got a man in mind for the job."

The barman grunted softly and asked, "Anybody I know?"

"I'm hoping so. Karl Hix. He used t' live here. I heard he's come back an' I'm wantin' to see him, see if he can do this thing for me."

"I'm not sure I know him. Hix, you said?"

"There would be, like, a finder's fee in it for you if I do find the man," Longarm said.

The barman leaned down onto his forearms resting on the bar. Longarm could practically see the thought processes working inside the man's brain. "How much?" The question was not exactly unexpected.

"Don't be greedy," Longarm told him. "We'll discuss that after you get me in touch with Hix."

"He a friend of yours?"

Longarm shook his head. "Friend of a friend. You know how that goes."

"I'm not saying that I know the man. But maybe I can get a message to him for you."

"A message is all I'm asking."

"If I do, it'll be up to him if he wants to meet with you."

"I understand that."

"Come back here tomorrow afternoon about two o'clock. That's a slow time in here, before the shifts change out at the mills and while they're still busy unloading ore cars over there. If Hix wants to see you, that would be the time he'd want to do it."

"If you happen to get the message to him."

"Right. If."

Longarm slid a silver dollar across the counter to pay for the beer that was sitting untouched on the bar in front of him. "Thanks for the beer."

He touched the brim of his hat and left, hoping he had not just wasted some of the taxpayers' money.

# Chapter 12

"Longarm, you are a dear sweet man and I love you to pieces, but sometimes I swear you are a bull in a china shop."

"What the devil are you talkin' about, Ginny?" He eyed the last bite of gravy-smothered chicken on his plate, contemplated whether he could hold that little bit more, and plunged his fork into it. Ginny's cook could damn sure do his job.

"I'm talking about this man you are looking for."

"Karl Hix," Longarm prompted, smoothing his mustache and swallowing back an urge to belch.

"I told you I have eyes and ears all over this town. I wish you had waited for me to find him for you."

"You know where he is?" Longarm asked, leaning forward. He pulled an after-dinner cheroot from his pocket and nipped the twist off. Ginny's serving girl appeared at his elbow with a lighted match before he could bring out a lucifer of his own.

Ginny sniffed and tipped her head back. "I know where he isn't," she said.

"What's that supposed t' mean?"

"You spooked him, dear. He got word that somebody was here looking for him, and he caught the next train over to Colorado Springs. I tried to find out where he went after that, but the best I could come up with was that he got onto a southbound from there."

"That makes sense," Longarm said. "He wouldn't want to go back t' Denver. There's paper out for him there."

"If you had just let things be, sweetie, I could have spotted him for you. Now, it looks like he will have gotten outside the reach of my, shall we say, friends."

Longarm sighed. "Sorry 'bout that, Ginny. Next time I'll listen to what you have t' say."

"No, you won't. You are much too impetuous for that. But it is sweet of you to say it anyway."

Longarm grunted and took a drag on his cheroot. It tasted good. "South, you say." He mused aloud, "The man could've changed trains in Pueblo an' gone west along the Arkansas to Leadville. Or stayed with the main line an' gone south all the way to Trinidad."

"I would help you with it if I could, dear, but I've already told you everything I know."

"Ginny, you're a love." He stood and leaned over to plant a kiss on the old broad's powdered, floral-scented cheek.

"You will stay over until morning?" she asked.

Longarm shook his head. "I'll be heading over to the main line this evenin', I think. I want t' catch the ticket agent over there before he goes off duty if I can. Mayhap he remembers Hix an' can tell me where it is that I'm headed my own self."

"I understand. But you won't get away with this the next time you come. I'll want you to spend some time with me, dearie." She smiled. "You do brighten an old woman's life."

"You're a doll, Ginny, an' if you was thirty years younger . . ."

"I'd do it too. Now go on. You have some packing to do."

"Not really. I never unpacked."

"Yes, you did," Ginny told him.

"Par'n me?"

She gave him a rueful look and a shrug. "I had your things brushed and put in the wardrobe for you."

Longarm laughed. "All right. In that case, I reckon I've got some packin' t' do after all."

He gave Ginny another kiss on the forehead and headed upstairs to his room.

# Chapter 13

Rather than wait for a train, Longarm grabbed a hansom to make the short three miles over to the Denver & Rio Grande depot in Colorado Springs. It was nearly eight o'clock when he got there. Half a dozen people were loafing on the southbound platform waiting for the next train. One young man looked familiar, but Longarm could not remember where he might have seen the lad.

He dumped his saddle and carpetbag on the platform and walked over to the window to speak with the ticket agent. After flashing his badge, he said, "I need you t' help me find a fella name of Karl Hix. He's about so tall," he said, holding the flat of his hand to indicate someone about five and a half feet tall. "Built kind of stocky and he ain't known for his personal grooming, if you know what I mean. Prob'ly wearing a soft cap. I think he might've bought a ticket south but I don't know to where. I need you t' tell me, mister."

The ticket agent, a balding man wearing sleeve garters and a green celluloid eyeshade, shook his head. "Sorry, Marshal. I sell them tickets to wherever they want, but I hardly ever look at them." A smile flashed, exposing yellow teeth. "Unless it's a good-looking woman. I notice them sometimes."

"Don't we all," Longarm said. "I can't blame you for that. Are you sure you can't remember . . ."

"Pueblo," a voice cut in from behind him.

Longarm turned, annoyed. The speaker was the young man he'd noticed on the platform, the one who looked vaguely familiar. The young fellow was slender. He had blond hair and a closely trimmed beard. He was dressed in a finely tailored suit and a bowler hat. He carried a cane with a bird-head grip.

"If you want a ticket to Pueblo, I'm sure this fella will be glad t' sell you one, but you'll hafta wait your turn," Longarm snapped. "For right now, I'm talking with the gentleman."

"And I am trying to answer your question," the slender young fellow said. "The man you are asking about bought a ticket to Pueblo. He left on the five-ten southbound."

"How would you know that?"

"A friend told me."

Longarm frowned. "I've seen you someplace before."

"That's right, you have." The young man took his hat off and extended his hand to shake. "I'm Joseph West, by the way."

"Custis Long," Longarm said, accepting the offered hand and pumping it briefly.

"Could we step away from this window?" the young fellow suggested. "Over here perhaps?" He led the way toward the north end of the platform where there were no other people close by.

"Why would you . . . ?"

"You don't remember me, Marshal, but I know who you are. The man you are after killed my father. You were at the funeral. I saw you there when you went through the receiving line. We shook hands at the time."

"Your father? D'you mean Hix has killed somebody else too? I'm after him about murdering a man in Denver

58

name of Joe Templeton. Who was your pa an' why did Hix kill him? An' just when was it I'm s'posed to've been at his funeral?"

"Joe Templeton was my father," West said.

"Then who is your mother?"

"You know her, Marshal Long. Her name is Katherine Templeton. Kate."

"Oh yeah, I remember you now. But I don't understand. Why is your last name different from his?"

West's expression was stoic and somewhat distant when he said, "My father disowned me, Marshal. He was ashamed of me. As soon as I was old enough, I went away to be on my own. I now live in San Francisco. I changed my name to avoid embarrassing him any further. I hadn't seen him in years, but I did keep in touch with Mom by mail. They moved to Denver after I left home.

"I think . . . I think my dad didn't want to be around anyone who knew about me."

"I still don't understand," Longarm admitted.

"I am an embarrassment, sir, because I'm a queer. My father was ashamed of me. That does not mean that I did not love him. I did. Whatever he said or did, he was still my dad, and I loved him."

"And Karl Hix . . ."

"He murdered my father, Marshal. I intend to find the son of a bitch and kill him," Joseph West said with calm certainty.

# Chapter 14

"You can't go around just killing people, no matter how much they deserve it, Joe. You, uh, you don't mind if I call you Joe, do you?"

"As a matter of fact, I do mind. I prefer Joseph nowadays. It . . . separates me from Dad just that much more. Everyone called him Joe, even people who had barely met him. He was very . . . informal."

"He was a good man, Joseph." Longarm refrained from pointing out that even though Joe Templeton's son had fallen far from the family connection, he nevertheless kept Joseph in his new name. But then he freely admitted that he had loved his father.

"I know that, sir. He was good to almost everyone."

"Almost?"

"He thought if he beat me often enough and hard enough, he could change my tastes. He was wrong about that. That did not, however, stop him from trying."

"Another reason why you left home early," Longarm guessed.

Joseph West shrugged.

"I tell you what, Joseph. Your father is dead now and can't be hurtin' you no more. An' by my experience, which is more consider'ble than I ever hoped it t' be, right now your mother'd be needin' you. You oughta be up home in Denver givin' comfort to her instead o' down here on a fool's mission. After all, I'm on Hix's tail. I intend t' bring him in to stand trial for what he done to your pa."

"Yes, sir. You are correct on all counts."

"You'll be goin' back then?"

"No, sir. I will not."

"But you said . . ."

"I do not dispute your facts, sir, and I appreciate your advice. Truly I do. I just will not be taking it. But thank you for your suggestion."

Longarm frowned. "I can't stop you from gettin' on a southbound, Joseph. But I surely wish you'd take the next northbound an' go home to your ma."

"Yes, sir. Thank you, sir."

"But you still won't do it, will you?"

West said nothing. He only shrugged. When the southbound pulled in, Longarm noticed, West boarded a car behind the smoker where Longarm preferred to travel.


Pueblo had grown since the last time Longarm was there. Again. It seemed the town was determined to make itself into a city. It had been a trading post, then a collection of adobe houses. Now Colorado Fuel & Iron had an ironworks there, turning out rails for the Denver & Rio Grande and burning coal dug by CF&I at the Ludlow mines down near Trinidad. The jump from a trading post set beside the Arkansas River to a bustling mill town was not an easy one. Longarm was glad he was not responsible for policing the streets here on a Saturday night.

This weekday night was bad enough. He could hear shouts and laughter and raucous music coming from the streets close to the railroad depot.

Gas lamps—those were new too—offered light along the public thoroughfares.

Longarm walked back to the baggage car to claim his gear, then shouldered his saddle and headed up the street. There was a hotel he had stayed at twice before and liked. It . . .

"Shit!" he grumbled aloud. The old Riverton Hotel was gone.

It hadn't just changed hands or been renamed. The whole damn structure was simply . . . gone. The Riverton had been torn down. By the light coming off the street lamps, he could see that work had begun on a building to replace it, although what that building would eventually be he had no idea.

Longarm paused on the sidewalk close to the new foundation and set his saddle and carpetbag down. He lighted a cheroot to give himself time to think.

Then he smiled.

He knew where he could get a good night's sleep. And more if he so chose.

He shouldered his gear again and set out at a brisk pace.

# Chapter 15

She called herself Jasmine DuVore, but her real name was Hilda Regnvald. When Longarm first met her, she was nineteen years old and had been whoring for eight of those years. She said her father was a northwoods lumberjack who started taking her into his bed when she was eleven. She ran away and went into the only trade she knew.

Did damned well at it, he guessed, with that mass of blond hair, innocent baby-blue eyes, kissable lips . . . and tits the size of melons. *Water*melons. There was something special about Hilda, though, the most amazing thing being that he actually believed the things she told him. But he did. He couldn't help it. She was direct and matter-of-fact. And not seeking anything from him.

They had been trapped together in a snowbound stage station for two days, and the confidences Hilda shared then rang true to him.

She was bright and she had plans for the future. If only she could find the financing, she intended to open a house where the gents would get a fair shake. No knockout drops. No lifted wallets. No clap. And the girls would get to keep an honest share of their earnings.

Those things, she explained, were so uncommon that she had never personally seen them.

Longarm liked her. So much so that when the road was cleared and they could travel on, he took Hilda back to Denver with him and introduced her to some gents with money in their pockets. They gave Hilda the financial backing she needed to buy a house here in rapidly growing Pueblo and stock it with top-quality girls and liquor that was not watered. The last Longarm heard from any of her investors, every penny had been paid back already. With interest.

When her deal with the Denver investors worked out, Hilda told him he would always be welcome in her house. On the house. His money would not be good there.

That shouldn't count as a bribe, he figured, because there was nothing Hilda wanted from him. And if someone wanted to object, well, hell, a man can't hardly help but have friends, and friends do for one another. That is just the way it is.

Hilda's place was situated on a knoll overlooking the Arkansas River valley and the lights of the city. To the south, there was fire and smoke coming from the iron-works even at this late hour. The town smelled of coal smoke. And money. Wages for the working man and prof-its for the fat cats. Everybody won.

Longarm paused on Hilda's front porch to finish a che-root and admire the view, then turned and tugged the bell-pull.

A peephole was opened first. Then the door was flung wide and a bundle of blond energy leaped on Longarm like a lioness taking down a fawn. If the girl had been ten pounds heavier, she likely would have taken him off his feet.

"Custis! Bay-bee! I am so glad to see you, bay-bee." Hilda draped herself over him, arms around his neck, legs clamped tight on his waist, and began kissing his neck and right ear. "Are you horny, bay-bee? I don't do gentlemen clients no more, but for you I go back in the business." She kissed him again.

"Hilda, they tore down the old Riverton and I was thinkin', well . . ."

"Bay-bee, this house is yours." Hilda turned and rang a delicate little bell that she carried in a pocket on her gown. A young maid appeared almost instantly. "Daisy, sweetheart, I want you to take Mr. Long's things to the Red Room for me. Unpack for him. Then let all the ladies know that the Red Room is occupied until further notice."

"Hilda, I don't want t' put you out or . . ."

"Now you just hush yourself, Custis. I love you dearly, and anything I can do for you will only be a joy. You couldn't put me out if you tried." She turned her attention back to the maid. "Go along now, dear."

"Yes'm." The girl dropped into a nice curtsy, then hurried to wrestle Longarm's gear away from him and carry everything up the stairs.

Longarm watched her go—she was stronger than she looked and had no trouble getting it all up the steps—then said, "That one's a mite young, ain't she?"

"That one will never have to service a gentleman caller if I have any say in it, bay-bee. Daisy is a sweet girl and I agree she is much too young to be in the life. I won't put up with that sort of thing in my house."

Hilda broke into a big grin. "Can you believe it, bay-bee. *My* house! Oh, how I like the sound of that."

"You're doing all right then?"

Hilda threw her arms out wide and spun around, her skirts flaring. "More than just all right, Custis. I'm doing wonderfully well." She chuckled. "All the other managers in town are jealous. They all think I have some great secret that brings the gentlemen back to me. I tell them it is simpler than they think. I run a clean, honest place. That's all the secret there is." She laughed. "They don't believe

67

me. They insist there has to be more to it than that. But there isn't."

She linked her arm through his and began leading him into a nicely appointed parlor where a dozen or more men milled around enjoying a drink or a conversation with one of Hilda's lovelies. There seemed to be five or six of those, all of them nicely dressed.

Even the gentlemen callers were clean and fairly well dressed, although several of them looked to be working-men rather than bosses. When Longarm remarked on that later, Hilda told him that one of her rules was that a gentle-man had to be bathed and in clean clothing or she would not allow him in.

"I can remember the stink of men who only bathed once or twice a year, and what it was like to be underneath them with my nose pressed up against their sweaty chest hair. The worst were the ones who wanted me to suck them when they probably hadn't washed their cocks since their mamas quit bathing them. I didn't do it, of course. I insisted they let me wash them first. But believe me, that got me an awful lot of hits upside my head."

"Hilda, I'm right proud o' the distance you've come an' the business you've built here. Proud t' call you my friend." He gave Hilda a hug and a light kiss on her forehead.

"Bay-bee, you don't know how much that means to me. What can I get you? Whiskey? A cigar? I have the best. But don't you dare ask me for a girl. You are mine, bay-bee. All mine."

# Chapter 16

It was a terrible loss to all of mankind the day Hilda Regnvald quit whoring. The girl—he could call her a girl, she
was still only in her mid-twenties—was just plain good.

"Lie still now, bay-bee." She giggled. "If you can."

Longarm was naked, skin still damp from a bath, lying
stretched full length on the huge feather bed in the Red
Room. Red indeed: walls, drapes, lamp shades, and even
the sheets were a deep bloodred. Hilda left the lamp burning, which lent an overall rosy tint to everything.

"No, dear. Roll over. On your tummy."

Longarm did as she asked.

"Now close your eyes, bay-bee."

He relaxed, all the tensions of the day leaving him as he
felt Hilda's tongue play inside his ear, then move around to
the back of his neck.

"You like, bay-bee?"

"Mm-hmm."

She laughed. "I thought you would." The tongue returned.
He could feel it, oh, so very well as it roved lightly across his
back and down his spine.

The bed tilted just a little when Hilda sat up. He thought
she was done with that very pleasant exercise and started

to roll over, but she stopped him with a whispered warning. "I'll be just a second here, bay-bee."

He felt more movement; then she leaned forward and deposited a handful of U-shaped hairpins on the bedside table. When she returned her attention to him, he could feel the cool brush of her hair on his skin in addition to that mobile tongue.

The girl continued down his spine to his butt, which she lingered over, sliding her tongue into the crack of his ass and damn near driving him crazy when she played the tip of it around and around his asshole.

"Jeez, girl."

Hilda laughed and tugged at his hip, urging him onto his back. When he rolled over, his cock—which felt like it was about to burst—and balls were close beneath her chin.

"Lovely," Hilda breathed, so softly he could scarcely hear.

She took hold of his cock and squeezed, pushing it back so that it was out of the way and his balls were lifted.

There was that tongue again. She licked his balls and gently sucked first one and then the other into her mouth.

"You don't know . . ."

"Shh! Hush, bay-bee."

Hilda raised up and shifted forward a little until her pretty face was poised above his pulsing rod. Then she opened her lips and dropped her head down onto him. Engulfing him in wet heat. Trying to suck the juice out of his body.

"I think . . ."

And then she was gone again. She sat up, smiling. Lordy, she was a pretty thing. Slim waist. Slim legs. Heart-shaped face with a perky nose and full lips. And those massive, pink-tipped jugs.

"Damn," he mumbled.

Hilda raised herself into a crouch and straddled his body, one foot planted on each side of his waist. She took his cock in both hands and held it in place as she guided herself down onto it. Her pussy was wet and so hot it felt like it was on fire. She took all of him into herself, something that not every girl could manage.

As he slid deeper and deeper within her body, Hilda's head sagged back and her eyes lost their focus and drooped almost shut. "Oh, I do love this, bay-bee," she whispered.

Then she began to grind, her thighs bumping against his sides and her ass slapping against his pelvis.

Longarm closed his eyes again and gave himself over to the pleasures Hilda was giving him.

# Chapter 17

The house was closed up and quiet when Longarm went downstairs about dawn to see if he could rustle up some grub for breakfast. There was a lingering scent of perfume, face powder, and cigar smoke in the air, but the place might have been empty for all the activity that was going on at this hour.

He found his way to the kitchen and discovered Hilda there, poring over a set of books laid out on the table with a coffee cup at her elbow. Longarm took a mug down from the china cabinet and poured himself a cup of stout coffee. He laced it with canned milk and sugar, then carried it to the table. He pulled out a chair and rubbed his eyes and face. He needed a shave, no two ways about it.

Yawning, he said, "You're up early."

Hilda smiled. "No, bay-bee. You are up early. Me, I'm still up from last night. The last of my girls just got in. I never go to bed until everyone is safe."

Longarm sipped at his coffee. It wasn't bad, but . . . "Listen, you wouldn't happen t' have, uh . . ."

Hilda laughed and left the kitchen. She was back moments later with a bottle of top-quality rye whiskey. She pulled the cork, laced his coffee with a dollop of the good rye, shrugged, and added a jolt to her own cup too.

"I've been thinking," she said after she sat again, "about this man you are looking for. You say his name is Hix?"

"That's right."

"What else can you tell me about him?"

"Why in the world would you want t' know that?" Longarm countered.

"I have contacts in this town, you know. Perhaps I can help. If he applies for work at the steel mill, I know I can find him for you. If he is just a saloon slacker"—she shrugged—"maybe not. I don't know. I'm not very popular with the saloon keepers in town. I take too much business away from them. A few of the bartenders owe me favors, though. Give me a few hours to get some sleep, then I'll ask around. See if I can turn up something about this Hix. So what else can you tell me about him?"

Longarm gave her a brief description of the SOB.

"You say he is wanted for murder?"

"Officially, he's suspected of robbing the mails. That makes it a fed'ral offense an' that means as a fed'ral deputy I can go after him. Actually, I want t' nail him for the murder of a barber back in Denver."

"Did he really rob the mail?" Hilda asked.

"Shit, no," Longarm admitted. "But don't expect me t' tell that to my boss."

"You are a scoundrel, Custis Long." Hilda laughed. "That is only one of the reasons I love you." She winked. "You and that hammer you carry between your legs. Damn, you're good." For a moment, she seemed dreamy-eyed and lost in a world of her own. Remembering perhaps. Then she smiled and stood. "Let me make us some breakfast. Then you can go off to, well, to whatever it is that you do when you are involved in these things. And I need to get some sleep before I can do you any good toward finding this Hix person."

"I can afford t' go out an' buy a breakfast, Hilda. No need for you t' be put out."

"Don't you know that it will be a pleasure for me to serve you, dear?"

He was not entirely sure how he should take that. But she certainly sounded serious when she said it. He hoped Hilda was not reading more into this visit—and the time they had spent together during the night—than was there.

"How do you want your eggs, dear? And would you rather have pork chops or sausage with them?"

"Uh, sunny-side up, I reckon. An' sausage. Maybe some fried taters if that wouldn't be too much bother."

"Then that is what it shall be. For you, dear, nothing is too much bother."

# Chapter 18

The only barbershop he could find was crowded and noisy, and he did not much feel like cozying up shoulder-to-shoulder with a bunch of strangers. He walked around a bit instead, marveling at the way Pueblo had changed since he first knew it.

The town used to be an adobe outpost where traders and sheepherders and a few garden truck farmers gathered for mutual protection against the local Indians. Now it was an industrial town with buildings constructed of milled lumber and even brick, those being possible now that the railroad was available for heavy hauling.

One of the more pleasant consequences of modern transportation was that now even good whiskey was cheap. It used to be that the only cheap whiskey was made of river water, alcohol, and rattlesnake heads.

It was a little early for any more rye, though, so Longarm ambled along until he found a tobacconist and stepped inside.

"Mornin'," he said. "D'you have any Hernandez y Hernandez?"

"Friend, I never even heard of them things. They a seegar?"

"Yes, sir, the best."

The proprietor shrugged. "I wisht I could help ya. But I got some good smokes here. I tell ya what. Try one that I'll recommend. If you don't like it, smoke it anyway on me. If you do, then pay me for it."

"Can't ask fairer than that," Longarm said. "Trot one of them things out for me."

The gent in sleeve garters and eyeshades brought out an apple-wood keg and opened it. The keg probably held a hundred or more cigars when it was full. Now there were less than half that on hand. The cigars were plump and dark-skinned. They smelled faintly sweet.

The fellow used a bronze cutter to clip both ends, handed the cigar to Longarm, and struck a match, allowing the sulphur to burn off before he offered it. Longarm dipped his head to put the end of the cigar in the flame and drew the smoke in.

"Nice," he said after a few moments. "Smooth and light." He smiled. "You've made a sale, mister."

"They're ten cents apiece," the gent warned.

"I'll take a dollar's worth." He handed over a cartwheel and put the other nine cigars into the side pocket of his coat. "Thank you, sir." Longarm touched the brim of his hat and wandered back out into the morning sunlight. If it was anything to judge by, this would be a mighty hot day. A glance over his shoulder, though, suggested there was little chance of rain any time soon.

Longarm enjoyed a two-cigar walking tour through Pueblo without encountering Karl Hix. He made a wide circle that brought him back to the barbershop where he had started. Most of the customers had been taken care of by then. There were only three men waiting for the two chairs in the shop when Longarm returned.

"You're next, mister," the Mexican barber closer to the front door said in a heavily accented voice.

Longarm looked at the others who were already waiting. "He means next after us," one of the men said.

Longarm nodded and took his hat off, hanging it on the polished walnut tree in a corner. He loosened his tie and unbuttoned his vest before picking up a dog-eared copy of the *Rocky Mountain News*. The paper was more than a week old and he had already read it back in Denver, but he did not mind. There were bound to be articles in there that he had not gotten to the first time through. He settled into a chair, crossed his legs, and opened the paper.

Twenty minutes or so later, the second chair came open and the barber—who apparently had no English, but who could whistle and snap scissors with the best of them— motioned Longarm into it.

Longarm shifted around a bit trying to get comfortable, but he was concerned that his Colt might bend those good cigars in his coat pocket, and he surely did not want to risk breaking the wrapper leaf on any of them. He tried moving the holster to the right, but that dug into his belly much too hard for comfort. If he moved it around to the left, it jabbed him in the ribs. And taking the coat off would require standing up and removing the striped sheet the barber had already draped over him. He settled for unbuckling his gunbelt and handing it to the barber. "Take care o' this for me, will you, *por favor?*" Lest the fellow misunderstand, he motioned toward the coat tree.

The barber smiled and bowed and draped the gunbelt over an arm of the coat tree, then returned to the serious business of Longarm's shave.

It was no wonder these two were so popular in the mornings. They had some little charcoal-fired pottery thing that kept their lather soothingly warm and turned a simple shave into a true pleasure. A shave here, Longarm figured, would be a bargain at twice the usual rate.

He leaned back and let the feathery touch of the barber's blade lull him half asleep.

Only half, though.

He could see through lowered eyelids when someone tall and burly came in. The new arrival sat and crossed his legs. He looked around. And then he snapped bolt upright in his chair.

"Long!" he blurted.

Longarm's eyes snapped open. Obviously, this fellow recognized him, but Longarm had no idea in hell who the man was. He did not even look vaguely familiar.

"Who're you?"

The man didn't answer, staring intently at Longarm. And then, with a quickly spreading smile, he glanced at the gunbelt that was hanging on the coat tree.

The gun had to be Longarm's as he was the only other customer in the place at the moment.

The smile became a huge grin, accompanied by an exultant cackle. "You son of a bitch!" he roared.

"Mind if I ask you . . . ?"

"You bastard! You cocksucker. You dirty, stinking cop."

"Look, if all you want t' do is insult me, I'm gonna have t' object an' ask you to stop it," Longarm said, not yet really pissed off. After all, he had been cussed many and many a time, but none of the words had yet torn any chunks out of his hide.

"Oh, I ain't gonna just in-*sult* you, Long. What I am gonna do is kill your fucking ass."

"Now, mister, I don't wanta ruin all this fun you seem t' be havin' at my expense, but I really do hafta draw the line there. Cuss an' rail all you like, but no shootin'."

"Oh, there is gonna be shootin'," the man chortled. "Oh, yeah. Lots an' lots of shootin'." He stepped over to place himself between Longarm and the coat tree where Longarm's Colt hung, then reached into his coat and pulled out a short-barreled revolver.

"I am gonna kill you, motherfucker, so close your eyes and start prayin'."

Longarm could see the fellow's finger begin to squeeze and the hammer on his snub-nosed revolver begin to roll back.

# Chapter 19

The front of the striped sheet covering Longarm billowed outward and a wisp of smoke escaped from a hole that was newly created there. The sharp, brittle report was muffled, however, by the linen.

The man who claimed he was going to kill Longarm coughed. He looked down at his shirtfront where a small, dark hole had suddenly appeared. It took a few moments before a trickle of blood began seeping out and staining his shirt.

"How . . . ?"

Longarm pushed the sheet aside—the damn thing had burst into flame and he did not want to singe his vest—revealing the little, brass-framed .41 derringer he wore as a watch fob. The pipsqueak pistol was cocked and ready for a second shot if one were needed.

"Jeez, I . . ." The would-be killer turned pale and his eyes lost their focus. Moving cautiously, as if afraid to lose his balance, he turned slowly around. He took a step forward, then reached for the wall to steady himself. Except the wall was a good six feet away. He went crashing face-forward onto the barbershop floor amid the clippings of hair and flecks of drying shaving soap.

The fellow's revolver clattered onto the hard surface. The impact of the fall dislodged the trigger sear, and the cheap revolver fired. Recoil from the gunshot sent the little nickel-plated weapon skittering away, spinning around and around until it finally came to rest underneath one of the waiting-area chairs.

Longarm jumped out of the barber chair and retrieved the dropped revolver before he did anything else. Once that was safely in his pocket, he took his own gunbelt down from the coat tree and buckled it on.

Then, but only then, he uncocked the derringer and slipped it back into his vest pocket.

Finally, he knelt to take a look at the man who lay on the floor, curled tight with his knees drawn up to his chest. He seemed to still be breathing.

"Who the hell are you, mister, and why'd you go an' do such a dumb-ass thing as that?"

The man blinked but did not speak. His breathing was ragged and shallow.

Longarm looked up at the barber. "D'you know this fellow? D'you know who this man is?"

The barber looked back at him blankly. And in fact may well not have had enough English to understand the question to begin with.

A stray thought reminded Longarm that at least the wound inflicted by the derringer was not bleeding much. The barbers would not have all that much blood to clean up.

"Why'd you try an' shoot me, you asshole?" Longarm gripped the fellow's shoulder and shook him a little to emphasize the question.

The man screamed and clutched himself all the tighter.

"Tell me, damn you." Longarm repeated the process of shaking the wounded man.

The fellow screamed again.

"Don't be such a pussy," Longarm grumbled. "You ain't dying."

The man blinked. After a moment, his eyes swiveled upward so he could see Longarm. "I'm not?"

"No, dammit, you aren't gonna die from a little puncture like that."

The man's hands relaxed slightly and his legs straightened just a little. "I'm not . . . not dying?"

"Shit, no. Likely you woulda been hurt worse if the barber nicked your chin this mornin'."

"I thought . . ."

"Yeah, I know what you thought. Now tell me who you are an' whyfor you went an' tried t' shoot me."

"My name . . . name is . . . Daniel Shay. I'm wanted . . . wanted . . . for murder . . . in Georgia."

"I hate t' add insult to injury, Daniel, but I never heard o' you."

"I thought . . . I saw you in Denver. Last week. A man . . . pointed you out. Said you were a deputy. You looked . . . looked my way. I thought . . . thought maybe you recognized me. From the posters. That's why"—he took a ragged breath—"why I run off. Came down here. Then today . . . this morning . . . I thought . . . thought sure you'd come . . . down here . . . after me. Thought sure."

"Well, you thought wrong, Daniel Shay. I never seen any posters on you an' wouldn't of knowed you from Adam's house cat."

"Shit," Shay said with considerable feeling. After a moment, he added, "Do you say I am not dying?"

"Oh, I'm sure you'll die someday, Shay. We all do eventually. Leastways, I never heard no way t' avoid it. But I don't think you're dyin' today."

Shay managed a smile. It was weak, but it was a smile. "Thank you."

That seemed a strange enough comment. But then dying men do and say strange things. And Daniel Shay was clearly spending his last moments on earth. Longarm's bullet had ripped through his vitals and the life was quickly seeping out of him now.

"Are you hurtin'?" Longarm asked. "Is there anything I can do for you whilst we wait for the doctor t' get here?" Not that a doctor had been called. There did not seem much point in it. An undertaker would suffice.

"No, I . . . I'm feeling easier. Now. A little light-headed. But it doesn't . . . doesn't hurt."

"That's good." Behind Longarm, the Mexican barbers were gabbling away at each other, but he had no idea what they were saying. Then one of them grabbed his coat and hat and headed outside. Likely, he would be going for either a doctor or the law, Longarm figured. Either or both would be fine. But Lordy, he hoped there would not be a lot of paperwork to fill out over this.

"Did José close the . . . close the curtains?"

"Why d'you ask?"

"Dark. Getting dark."

"Yeah, he pulled the shades down," Longarm lied. "So's folks wouldn't stare in at you through the window."

"Thought . . . ful." Shay's voice was very weak and small.

"Yeah, José is plenty thoughtful," Longarm said.

Shay's mouth worked as if he were trying to say something, but whatever it was never got said. After another few moments, his eyes rolled back in his head and his hands fell away from his midsection.

Longarm reached down and touched Shay's eyeball. There was no blink reaction.

Longarm stood, his knee joints creaking, and walked around behind the barber chair to take a towel off the shelf and begin wiping the rest of the lather from his face. There would be no finishing his shave. Not in this shop anyway. Not today.

Then he sat down to wait for the local law to arrive.

# Chapter 20

"I've heard of you, Long." The uniformed policeman stuck his hand out. "Pleased to meet you, sir."

"My name ain't 'sir.' I expect you can call me Longarm. Most everyone does," Longarm said, shaking the officer's hand. He felt a little uncomfortable being addressed as "sir" by someone who was obviously older than he was. The Pueblo policeman was probably in his fifties, judging by outward appearances.

"They call me Outlaw," the policeman said.

Longarm raised his eyebrows. There had to be a tale behind a nickname like that.

"My name is Harold James," Outlaw explained.

"An' folks right off go t' thinkin' you must be kin to Frank an' Jesse, is that it?"

"Yeah, and the truth is that they are right. We're distant cousins. So . . ." He shrugged.

"We all got our crosses t' bear," Longarm said. "Getting back t' this incident, though . . ." He went on to fill in Outlaw James on the little he knew about Daniel Shay and the facts that had led to his death.

When Longarm was done, Outlaw whistled. "You were lucky, him coming at you like he did."

Longarm grunted. "Wasn't no luck involved, Outlaw. What I was was ready. There's a difference."

"I am sure you're right," James said, although his tone of voice suggested that might not be entirely true. He shuddered and made a face. "I surely am glad I don't have your job, though. Hauling the drunks off the streets on Saturday nights is one thing. Living like you do is something else entirely." The officer smiled. "Remind me to light a candle in gratitude come Saturday confession. If you like, I will light one for you too."

"That'd be real nice o' you." Longarm could not quite see the connection. But then he was not Catholic and probably could be forgiven that lack of comprehension. What he could understand was that he had not yet reloaded his derringer.

He had a few spare cartridges for the seldom-used little gun, but they were in his carpetbag back at Hilda's whorehouse. At least, hmm, he thought he had some spares. If he remembered to transfer them the last time he traveled with just his saddlebags. Damn! The more he thought about it, the less sure he was. He thought about it a few moments longer, then asked Outlaw James, "Where can I buy ammunition? It's an odd size, so just everybody might not carry it."

The policeman pointed. "Two blocks down, then one over to your right. The department gets a discount there. Show your badge and I'll bet you can get one too."

"Thanks." Longarm pulled out a pair of cigars and offered one to Outlaw, then trimmed his own and lighted both off the same match. "D'you need me here any longer?"

James shook his head. "I can take care of it, but it would help if you'd stop by City Hall late this afternoon. I'll have a statement ready for you to sign. We are in the basement."

"Ain't that just the way things are," Longarm said. "The politicians get the glory an' the good views out the windows. Us peacekeepers get whatever is left over that they don't want."

Outlaw grinned and spread his hands in a "what can you do" gesture.

"I'll see you later," Longarm said. He touched the brim of his hat and headed off in the direction Outlaw had indicated.

The brief walk ended at a gunsmith's shop. The shop had heavy bars on the lone window in front and the door as well, but the proprietor looked like he did not have a care in the world. Of course, those bars blocking thieves might have contributed to that lightheartedness. "How can I help you?" he asked when Longarm came in, his entrance accompanied by the chiming of a little bell suspended overhead.

Longarm explained his need and added, "Officer James said I might get a professional discount from you like the local coppers do."

"Are you a policeman?"

"Not 'zac'ly." Longarm flipped his wallet open to display his federal badge. "Custis Long. I work for Billy Vail up to Denver."

*"Longarm?"* the gunsmith enthused. "Gracious, I . . . you are one of my heroes. May I shake your hand? And perhaps an autograph? Would you mind doing that? Oh, my!"

Longarm provided both the handshake and the signature and protested—but to no avail—when the gunsmith refused to accept payment for a full box of .41 rimfire cartridges.

"What brings you to our fair little Pueblo?" the smith asked while he wrapped Longarm's cartridges in heavy paper and tied the package with string.

"Lookin' for a fugitive, o' course," Longarm said. "Fella name of Hix."

"Karl Hix?" the smith said, looking up from his task.

"That's right. D'you know him?"

"I . . . I hope I didn't do anything wrong," the gunsmith said. "Just this morning, I sold him a revolver. A Remington .44 Army that has been converted to use cartridges."

"Did he say what his plans are? Or why a small-time alley cat like him would want a grown man's handgun?"

The man shook his head. "No. I wish I could help you, but no."

"Did he say where he's staying now he's back in town?"

Again, the shake of the man's head. "I'm sorry, no." After a moment, the fellow said, "But I think I've seen the other man down by the tracks once or twice before."

"Other man? There was someone else with him?"

"Yes. A man named . . . I don't remember for sure. Blake, I think. That could be his last name or his first. I just don't know."

"Outlaw James and his pals might know where this Blake lives. Reckon I'll ask them. And thanks, friend. You been a real help. I appreciate it. Now one more thing, if you don't mind. What's the best way t' get to City Hall from here?"

The gunsmith leaned forward over his counter and pointed. "You go down that way and . . ."

# Chapter 21

"Sure, I know him. Blake Richards. He's about your age. A little taller maybe. Wears his hair buffalo-hunter style, down on his shoulders. That shit makes a man look like a woman far as I'm concerned. I've no idea what he does for a living, although he always has a dollar to spend on a drink or a doxie. Or two. He's the sort would go for the fifty-cent whores or the two-bit señoritas. I know I don't like standing downwind from the son of a bitch. But where he lives"—Outlaw shrugged—"I've never cared to ask. We can step around and talk to the jailer. He might know. The man is in and out of the pokey pretty regular for public intoxication and small shit like that. Or Tom might know if some bail bondsman stood good for him and the bondsman could tell you that address."

Longarm followed Outlaw through a corridor and a heavy, iron-reinforced door to the basement jail area where patent-steel cages had been installed, complete with steel-plate ceilings. The floors and walls were solid stone. Stone can be tunneled through, of course, but not without the effort becoming very quickly visible from outside the cells.

The jailer was introduced only as Tom, no last name given. He was a gray-haired old cuss who looked like he had seen all the sass he intended to stand for and would not take any more. Not from any-damn-body.

Tom shook his head when Longarm's and Outlaw's question was posed. "Nope. I got no idea. Richards never posts bond. I ast him about that once. He said it'd add up to cost too much if he got to posting bond or paying somebody to do it for him. Besides, he said, he don't mind spending a night or two on a good bed."

Longarm glanced into the nearest cell. The bed there was a steel shelf bolted to the wall with a thin mattress and one long blanket laid over it. If this was what Blake Richards thought of as a "good" bed, what the hell sort of bed was he normally accustomed to?

"Wish I could help you," Tom said.

"You can't tell what you don't know. Any guesses where he might spend his time?"

"Not me. I never spent no time visiting with him. The man don't bathe regular, and I'm not keen on being around him."

"All right, thanks." Longarm shook the man's hand, then followed Outlaw back to the police officers' briefing room. There was a large chart tacked up on the wall. According to that, crime in Pueblo was on the increase. "That due t' the steel mills?" Longarm asked, nodding toward the chart.

"Sure. More people means more crime. We try to hold it down, though. It's mostly petty stuff. If you look close there, you'll see that we don't have much murder for a town this size, and those are just the usual sorts of thing that you can't avoid anyway. Lovers' quarrels and shit like that." Outlaw chuckled. "I sometime think if it wasn't for liquor and love, the likes of you and me would be out of business."

Longarm laughed. "Damn if you ain't right about that." He stuck his hand out. "If you'll excuse me, I'd best see if I can turn up anything about my boy Hix."

"If I should happen to run across anything, Longarm, where can I find you to pass the information along?"

"I'm staying at Hilda Regnvald's place."

"I don't think I know of anybody named Regnvald."

"Sorry. You probably know her as Jasmine DuVore."

Outlaw's eyebrows went up and he scowled disdainfully.

"She's an old friend," Longarm started to explain. Then he clamped his mouth shut. He did not owe Outlaw James any explanations, and if the fucker wanted to disapprove of his sleeping arrangements, well, piss on him. "Thanks for your help," he said curtly, then turned and left.

# Chapter 22

The only lead Longarm had as to the likely whereabouts of Blake Richards and/or Karl Hix was the gunsmith's offhand comment that he had seen Richards down by the railroad tracks a time or two. Pueblo being something of a railroad town, not to mention the steel mills, there were tracks in pretty much any direction a man might care to walk. And while that might be an exaggeration, it wasn't all that much of one. Longarm hitched up his britches and headed for the main north-south line of the Denver & Rio Grande.

He knew better than to try to ferret out every asshole who haunted the tracks. But he knew who might well be able to point him in the right direction.

He asked a few directions and wound up at the D&RG yardmaster's hut.

"You're in the wrong place, mister," he was told upon entry into the tiny, adobe brick building. "The passenger and freight depot is up that way 'bout a half mile. Just follow the tracks. You can't miss it." The fellow speaking was small, painfully thin, and wore a dark green celluloid eyeshade surrounding a nearly bald dome.

"Not if you're the yardmaster, I ain't." Longarm showed his badge and introduced himself. "I'd sure appreciate the help o' your railroad detectives," he said. "I'm lookin' for a couple fellas an' think they might be able t' point me in the right direction."

"May I see that badge, please?" The yardmaster might be on the small side of things, but he was not intimidated. He held his hand out with an air of authority. Longarm handed over his wallet with the badge pinned inside. The yardmaster took his sweet time inspecting the credentials, even taking the tin out of Longarm's wallet and turning it over to look at the back.

"What'd you do that for?" Longarm asked.

"Do what?"

"Turn my badge around like you just done."

The yardmaster permitted himself a small and satisfied smile. Then he began carefully returning Longarm's things to their original place and condition. "Counterfeiters," he said. "In my day, I've seen all manner of fakes. Fake tickets, fake badges, fake uniforms. Your typical counterfeiter would be careful with the surface of a phony badge. He would not be so likely to pay attention to the back. That is what I was looking for."

Longarm grinned. "I just learned something t'day. Thanks."

"Glad to be of service." The yardmaster stood and leaned across the desk to extend his hand to shake. "My name is Stokes. Now what is it that I can do for you, Marshal?"

"I'm lookin' for two fellas name of Karl Hix and Blake Richards, Mr. Stokes. I'm told they been known to loaf about along your tracks, mayhap in your yards. D'you know anything about them?"

"I do not, but some of my people might. Can you wait a few minutes?"

"O' course."

Stokes left his desk and went outside. He had a heavy limp and it looked like one of his legs was shorter than the other—perhaps it was artificial—but it was obvious that he did not allow that disability to hold him down.

He opened a wooden locker that was affixed to the side of the shack, selected a handful of colorful pennants, and used spring-loaded clips to hang them onto a flagpole. When he was satisfied with the display, he ran them up to the top of the pole, then tugged a bellpull that resulted in a screeching whistle blast.

Longarm winced, then when the shrieking ended, asked, "What the hell was that all about?"

"The whistle calls attention to the message I just displayed. My people all over the yard can see the pole. Those flags up there"—he pointed with his chin—"tell them who I want and where they should report. If there were a problem, I could tell them the nature of the trouble as well. But I don't have a flag"—he smiled—"to warn them a federal officer wants to talk with them."

"Good idea."

"I did not invent it myself." The smile briefly returned and then was gone again. "But I may have improved on it a little. Come inside. We can have coffee while we wait for my men to trickle in."

Stokes led the way back into the shack. Within minutes, the railroad detectives, all of them who happened to be in the Pueblo yard at the moment, began arriving.

"This is everybody," a tall, narrow-hipped man with a drooping mustache and a boxer's scarred hands said when five of them had squeezed inside the tiny office with Stokes and Longarm.

"Where is Mason?" Stokes demanded, his voice crisp.

"In town. He's checking to see if a crate was intact when it reached the consignee."

"All right. Everyone pay attention, please. This is Deputy United States Marshal Custis Long. He is asking for our help locating . . . what did you say those names were again?"

"Karl Hix. Blake Richards." Longarm gave a description of Hix. "I don't know Richards, but I'm told you probably do. The one I am looking for is Hix. I understand he has been seen in Richards's company lately. That's why I'm here."

"Yeah, we know that son of a bitch," another of the burly head-knockers growled.

"Useless bastard," another put in. "But he's always got brass in his pockets." That one had a British accent.

"What did you say your man Hix looks like again?"

Longarm told him.

The man who had asked the question nodded. "He was here. I seen the two of them together as recent as last night. Or this morning, more like, but well before dawn. They looked like they'd been off having more than a few drinks someplace."

"Do you know where they might be now?" Longarm asked.

"Richards mostly sleeps in a lean-to he built over in Fleatown."

"Fleatown," Longarm repeated. "I never heard of it."

Stokes smiled. "You would not have. It is the name we use for a squatters' camp where hoboes congregate. It is off the railroad right-of-way, so technically speaking we have no authority there, but . . ."

"You don't have t' explain yourselves t' me," Longarm said. "I understand how it can be."

"In that case, Jessup, why don't you take the marshal over to Fleatown and help him look for Richards and this Hix person. The rest of you can go back to what you were doing."

# Chapter 23

Jessup was a man who wore a bowler hat, likely as a deliberate taunt daring any son of a bitch to mock him for it. He looked like a man who enjoyed brawling, and he had the scars to prove it. He had red hair, a full beard, and muscles in places that Longarm was not entirely sure he had himself.

"I tried to get me a depitty marshal job," Jessup said conversationally as he led Longarm through the railroad yard, then west of the tracks toward the distant mountains. "Never got hired, though. You boys got to be good with your guns. Me, I couldn't hit.a bull in the ass with a bass fiddle. Seems these big ol' paws of mine don't fit around the butt of a pistol so good." He grinned. "They can manage an ax handle just fine, though."

"Tools of the trade," Longarm said. "We each got our own."

"Ain't that the truth. Right over this way now. Mind your step here."

"What, they got a bunch o' dogs in the camp?"

"Why do you ask that?" Jessup said.

"All the piles o' turds layin' everywhere."

"That ain't dogs. That's from the hoboes. They need to take a dump, they just drop their trou and turn loose. At least, most of them walk outside the camp to do it. Most, I said. Not all."

"Smells like an Indian camp," Longarm said. "Except Indians move their camps every now and then. Gives them fresh places to drop their shit."

"Over here," Jessup said, pointing.

Fleatown was a collection of shanties and tents made from broken crates, scraps of old canvas, and flattened sardine tins. There were more than a dozen of the makeshift hovels scattered around a central fire pit and a rubbish heap. A stink of feces, long-unwashed bodies, and wet ash hung over the place.

"Over this way, I think," Jessup said. "I seen Richards in one of these over here." He lifted the door flap on one of the flimsy structures and peered inside.

"Wha' d'you wan'?" a bleary-eyed hobo mumbled. "I ain't in yer stinkin' yard."

Longarm stepped forward, insinuating himself between the head-breaker and the hobo, smiling as he did so. "I'm looking for your help," he said. "I'm offering a reward."

The filthy, disheveled hobo sat up and rubbed his eyes. "What kinda reward?"

"First tell me what I need t' know," Longarm said.

"Whaz that?"

"I'm looking for two men. You know Blake Richards. There is a man with him, a man I need t' talk with. His name is Karl Hix. He's about so tall." He indicated it with the flat of his hand. "Dark hair."

"Shit," the hobo grumbled.

"Why d'you say that?"

"I can't tell you where they went. I dunno that."

"They were here, though?"

"Yeah, but I don' think they're coming back. That sonuvabish Richards dug up his money pouch an' took it

100

with him. Reason I say he ain't coming back is that he seen me watching an' didn't care that I knew where he'd kept it. Took his blankets too. Him and that other fella, whatever you say his name is."

"Hix," Longarm prompted.

"Yeah, him. I never met him, mind you. But he looks like you say and he's thick with that bastard Richards. Richards stole my bottle," the hobo complained. "Must of been near a pint left in 'at bottle too, damn him."

"But you don't know where they were going?" Longarm asked.

"Nope. I do know one thing. The direction they took from here, they likely was going up-canyon, up inta those mountains or at the least headed over that way."

"Why d'you say that?"

"The rails, mister. If they was going north or south, they could've hopped a freight on the main line. The direction they was going from here, that's the line up along the river to that place . . . uh, that place . . ."

"Buena Vista?" Longarm suggested. "Leadville?"

"Yeah. Up there. They was headed, like, toward that line."

"Thanks. You've been a big help." Longarm dug into his pocket for a Mexican silver peso and handed it to the man, then motioned for Jessup to walk with him. "When is the next westbound?" he asked.

"This afternoon," Jessup told him. "But if your men were going that way, they've probably already left. There was a fast freight running mostly empty cars that left this morning to pick up material from the mines up there."

"Shit," Longarm growled.

"They could be halfway to Salida by now."

"Shit," Longarm said.

"Hey, it ain't my fault if they've left."

"No, I meant it when I said shit. I stepped in some." He

paused to scuff his feet in the dirt to wipe some bum's shit off his boot.

"You got to watch your step around here," Jessup said.

Longarm was not sure if he was hiding a grin inside that beard or not. "*Now* you tell me," he said.

# Chapter 24

There was a mixed train—freight and passenger cars together—scheduled to pull out of Pueblo at 4:17 p.m. Longarm had plenty of time for a leisurely lunch before he headed for the depot, and he knew just who he would like to squire out on the town for a fancy meal.

"Hilda! Where the hell are you?" he roared when he strode through the vestibule at Madame DuVore's Whorehouse and on into the parlor. Hilda quickly appeared at the top of the stairs.

"Will you please be quiet? My ladies need their beauty sleep," Hilda chided, holding a finger to her lips.

"How can I be quiet when I see s' much beauty standin' there?"

Hilda glanced down at herself, then started to laugh. Unlike the glamorous impression she tried to make for her clients in the evenings when she dressed in flowing gowns and sparkling baubles, at this midday hour in the privacy of her home, she was wearing a shapeless and faded old housedress. And if Custis Long was any judge—and he certainly thought that he was—she did not have anything on beneath it. He could clearly see the pointed bumps made by her nipples pressing the fabric over her breasts.

"Beauty," she said. "You must be daft."

Longarm swept his hat off in a broadly theatrical gesture. "Made so by the force o' your loveliness," he agreed.

"Full of blarney too, my dear."

"Get dressed. I'm gonna squire you out on the town for lunch. On the gummint's tab too, so put your duds on," Longarm ordered from the bottom of the stairs. He leaned on the newel, as large and as round as a bowling ball, and rested a boot on the second step, grinning up the stairs at her. "Damn, you're a fine-lookin' woman, Hilda Regnvald."

"Come up and help me dress," she said.

"I'm already about wore out from what you done t' me last night, darlin'. Don't make me climb these steps now just so's you can come down 'em with me."

Hilda did not say anything, but she did step daintily to the head of the stairs. She gave him a cat-got-the-canary smile and spread the front of her housedress open. Sure enough, she was naked beneath the flimsy cloth.

"You ain't fightin' fair," Longarm complained.

"They will serve lunch whenever we manage to get there," Hilda said.

Longarm cleared his throat. Then practically leaped up the staircase to join her at the top. "You was sayin' something?"

She smiled again and twirled around, the flowery scent of her perfume floating in the air around her. Hilda reached up and crooked her finger before she disappeared into the bedroom that Longarm remembered so well—and so fondly—from the night before.

She stopped beside the big bed, still wearing that smile.

Then she shrugged the housedress off her shoulders, allowing it to slither quietly to the floor. She posed before him, hips turned, one knee slightly bent.

And she had that smile.

"Well?" she challenged.

"Damn!" Longarm mumbled. He stepped forward, and Hilda came into his arms. She tasted of mint and cloves, and her perfume was sweetly heady. "You do feel good in a man's arms," he breathed into her ear.

Hilda tipped her head back and raised her mouth to his. She pressed forward with her hips, grinding her belly into his belt buckle and holstered revolver. If she felt any discomfort, she did not show it. When she spoke, her voice was throaty and thick. "Fuck me. Please, dear. Fuck me now."

Longarm dropped his coat, then the gunbelt. Hilda helped him out of the rest of his clothing. Within moments, he was bare-ass naked, a throbbing erection poking Hilda in the stomach when again he embraced her.

"Don't wait. No foreplay," she urged. "Now. Fuck me now."

Longarm picked her up and dumped her onto the bed. Hilda swung one leg to the side and Longarm settled into the middle of her, plunging deep inside her already wet body.

She cried out as the length of his meat filled her, but soon her whimpering turned to purrs of sheer pleasure.

This, he thought at one point, was better than food any old time.

# Chapter 25

Longarm had to run like a hundred-yard sprinter to catch onto the ass end of the westbound train, and at that he had to settle for grabbing hold of the caboose. He threw his saddle and his carpetbag onto the platform, then accepted a hand up from one of the brakemen who had snuck out back to have a smoke.

"Thanks," he said, brushing himself off and kicking his gear away from the edge of the platform. It wouldn't much do for his things to fall off and go bouncing along the ties while he and the train disappeared toward the distant valleys and canyons of the Arkansas River.

"You got a ticket, mister? The boss, he ain't gonna like it if you don't got a ticket."

"I got a ticket, friend," Longarm assured the greasy, soot-stained fellow. "Tell me, is there a dining car on this train?" He was hungry. He had spent so much time being eaten by dear Hilda that he hadn't had time for eating the meal he'd promised her.

The brakeman looked at him like he was daft—and perhaps the question was—then answered, "No, of course not, but there's a kid somewhere up front selling samwidges and pies and shit."

"That should do. D'you mind if I leave my things back here until I get off?"

"I dunno if that would be all right or not."

Longarm pulled out his wallet and flipped it open to display his badge. "Trust me, friend. It will be all right."

"Oh, I . . . uh . . . yeah. Sure. I'll see to your stuff. Whenever you want it, just holler. I'll set it out for you."

"Thanks." Longarm gave the man a phony smile and resolved not to worry about whatever it was in the past that made the brakeman so eager to please now. And who knows, maybe it was simple helpfulness.

The brakeman set Longarm's gear inside the caboose while Longarm leaned out over the rail to take a look. There was no catwalk along the sides of the six freight cars so it looked like up-and-over was the only way to reach those passenger cars ahead.

He went forward through the caboose, then stepped across the coupling to the back of the last freight car and took the ladder to the top of the car. The empty car was bucking and rattling beneath his feet. Not exactly confidence inspiring. Still, if he wanted a bite to eat before he got to . . . where the hell was he going on this thing anyway? He still had not figured that out. It was not like Blake Richards and his new buddy, Karl Hix, had bought tickets to their destination. Riding the rods underneath the cars like they were, they could drop off anywhere the trains slowed. That was going to make it damned difficult to follow them. Still and all, he would do what he could and trust Dame Fortune to keep him on the right track.

Longarm took a few moments to become accustomed to the swaying, bumping surface under his boots, then started forward along the top of the freight car, having to step across the ventilators as he came to them. It was sort of like riding a bronc, he thought. But standing up on the seat of the saddle and with no reins to hang on to. If only he hadn't taken time to let Hilda wash all the sticky juices off him . . .

He stumbled once, righted himself, then hurried on to the front of that car. One down, five to go.

He climbed down the ladder, stepped across the coupling, and started up the next car.

By the time he reached the second of the two passenger coaches, he was quite heartily sick of the stink of the coal smoke that poured out of the stack on the engine. Past experience told him he would have the lingering smell inside his nose for days to come. A little coal smoke smelled just fine, especially on a crisp and invigorating winter's morning. But this . . . this was somewhat more than enough.

It was with considerable relief that he threw a leg over the rail on the platform behind the passenger car and stood on reasonably firm footing again for a change.

He reached for the door handle, intending to go forward into the car, but the door was pulled open before he could reach it.

Longarm found himself face-to-face with Joe Templeton's son, Joseph West.

# Chapter 26

"What are you doing here?" Longarm asked.

"Nothing illegal, Marshal. I'm just a citizen, traveling and enjoying the countryside."

"Bullshit!"

West smiled and spread his hands in a display of innocence.

"I won't allow vigilante justice, West. I want you t' know that. No matter what Hix has done, I won't be allowin' you t' play the vigilante."

"That's all right, Marshal. I'm not the type for it anyway."

Longarm motioned toward the seats. "D'you mind? I'm a little winded after runnin' over the top of this sonuvabitch train." He sat, reaching into his coat for a cigar and a match, and West settled onto the bench facing Longarm's.

"Tell me," Longarm said. "How'd you come t' learn about the man bein' headed this way?"

"I thought I told you before, Marshal. We perverts are a gossipy bunch. And we tend to help each other." West looked away, his expression bleak. "God knows we face enough troubles whenever we are found out. We try to help each other when we can."

111

"I can understand that," Longarm said, "but how the hell d'you find each other? I mean is there, like, a club or a signal, some sort o' sign or handshake like them Masons got?"

West laughed. There might have been a trace of bitterness in the sound. "No, nothing like that, Marshal. But there is . . . how can I explain this so you will understand . . . sometimes we can recognize each other when you straight people cannot. It is . . . a way of moving. A body awareness, you might say." He smiled and shrugged. "It is the sort of thing that makes us such good dancers and artists and actors, I think. And yes, certainly I've thought about it, wondered about it myself. All I can really tell you is that it is there. I can see it and feel it even if I cannot really understand it myself."

"That's interestin'," Longarm said, "but what's it got t' do with Karl Hix?"

"Someone . . . a part-time piano player in a saloon . . . overheard Hix and his new partner talking. They were planning a robbery. The other fellow recruited Hix to help him with it and said they would catch the morning westbound."

"Where's this robbery gonna be?"

"The piano player didn't hear that."

"Did he say anything to the police about it?"

"Of course not. We've pretty much learned to mind our own business and stay as invisible as we can, Marshal. When one of us is found out, it doesn't usually matter what we are doing. If anything. People call us names. Humiliate us. Beat us up. Sometimes worse. So we just keep our mouths shut regardless." The handsome young man grinned. "Well, except for, um, sometimes."

"You mean . . . ?" Longarm shook his head. "Christ, man, that ain't something t' joke about."

"I don't mean to make you uncomfortable. Perhaps we shouldn't talk about my kind. Getting back to the original subject, Marshal, my queer friend said nothing to the authorities, but when he learned of my interest in Hix, he sought me out and told me what he heard. Too late, unfortunately, for me to be on that same train, but hopefully in time for me to find them. Now may I ask you something?"

"Hell, you can ask anything. That don't mean you'll get an answer, but you can ask."

"How do you happen to be on this train?"

"Pretty much the same as you. I heard they was paired up an' headin' out this direction, so here I be."

"Do you know where they are going?"

"Not no more'n you do," Longarm said. "I wisht I did."

"So how will you go about finding them?" West asked.

Longarm smiled and puffed on his cigar. "Sheer, bull-headed persistence," he said. "It's the one tool the lawman has that a crook can't beat. We just keep a-comin' till the job is done, and if one of us can't do it, then another one will."

The train rattled across a culvert, trailing a plume of gray smoke.

# Chapter 27

If he had to personally talk to every son of a bitch who had been on every platform at every little whistle-stop between Pueblo and end-of-track that morning, well, that was just what he would have to do. Most citizens had no idea, but the vast bulk of law enforcement work consisted of plain old stubbornness.

"Staying with the train t' the other end?" Longarm asked West as the train rattled and clanked, slowing for the depot at Canon City.

"Not that far," the young man said. "I have a friend in Salida. He's pretty well connected. Officially and privately too. Once I talk with him, I should have a hundred eyes and ears primed to look for Hix and his friend Richards."

Longarm grunted, then stood as the train lurched to a halt. "I dunno if I should wish you luck or not. Truth is, you're a nice fella but you make me a mite uncomfortable. An' what you got it in mind t' do is against the law. Truth is, I hope the two o' us don't meet up again." Longarm touched the brim of his Stetson. "My respects t' your mama, Joseph."

"Thank you, Marshal. I will be sure to tell her that." The handsome young man smiled and offered his hand, his fingers barely touching Longarm's. "Good luck to you."

Longarm shrugged. "T' you too, son." He turned and headed toward the back of the passenger car, falling in line there with the others who were leaving the train at Canon City.

It was mildly puzzling why so many families carrying baskets of food with them would be leaving the train here. Then he realized. This must be a visiting day at Old Max, formerly the territorial prison and now Colorado's state penitentiary.

It occurred to him that Blake Richards and his new recruit could have come this way to meet a prisoner who was being released today. Longarm figured if he got no information at the railroad depot, he would try the prison next to see who might have been scheduled for release today and who, if anyone, had met them on their way out.

There were eight or ten people jammed up at the top of the steps, at least three families, the aging women carrying baskets—he could see sausages and pies and the like, typical treats a family might bring to a loved one behind bars—and worn-out men who looked like they long ago were beaten into submission by lack of rain and pests and falling prices in those rare years when they did bring in a good crop. God, Longarm was grateful he was able to escape from the grinding labor and the poverty of his West Virginia home. Else by now, he probably would have looked much like these men, stooped and aged before his time.

He waited patiently for them to disembark, one woman in particular holding things up. The poor thing had something wrong with her legs and whatever it was made her ankles and lower legs as thick as a nail keg. She looked like she was in pain. But he had to give the lady her due. She was determined to make that visit. And she had a full basket carried on her arm.

It took a while for her family to get her safely down onto the platform. As soon as there was room for him to follow, Longarm swung lightly down the steel steps.

"Boooo-ard!" the conductor called as he made his way back along the train. "All aboard for Howard, Salida, and Buena Vista. Boooo-ard!"

Before the last sounds even left the man's lips, the train gave a great clanking and rattle as the engine pulled forward and the steel couplings clashed together.

"All aboooo-ard!"

Longarm dropped off the train just as it began to move. He grinned and reached into his coat pocket for a cigar, and dipped into his vest for a match.

Time to go to work, he thought.

He was opening the door to the stationmaster's office when he glanced toward the train that was now gathering speed for the run into the mountains following the valley of the Arkansas River.

He saw . . . oh, *shit*!

What he saw was that sonuvabitch caboose rolling by.

With his saddle, carbine, and carpetbag helpfully stored inside it.

Shee-it!

# Chapter 28

The stationmaster shook his head. "Nobody by that description that I've heard of." His lips thinned in a wry smile. "Most generally the 'boes avoid Canon. Something to do with Old Max there, I suppose," he said, hooking a thumb in the direction of the high, cold, stone walls of the state penitentiary a few hundred yards west of the depot. "They all of them know they could end up inside. Gives them the shivers just to look at it. But I tell you what. I haven't spoken with all the men who were on shift this morning when that freight came through. Let me ask around. Maybe somebody saw something that I don't know about."

"I'd 'preciate it," Longarm told him.

"These men you're looking for. Are they likely to be coming back here in chains?"

"One of them is for sure. He's suspected of robbing the U.S. mail and he for damn sure murdered a man up in Denver. I suspect the U.S. attorney would let the state have first crack at him on the more serious charge. If I catch up with him . . . *when* I catch up with him . . . he's apt t' come back down here for a short walk on the gallows platform."

The stationmaster shuddered. "I was official witness to a hanging once. The sound of that trapdoor opening and that rope popping and then the neck breaking . . . Jesus, it makes me want to puke again just thinking about it now." His face turned pale, and Longarm almost thought that the man would throw up right there in his own comfortable office. "I can still see the way his legs kicked and smell his shit squirting out of him and running down inside his pants legs. Jesus God! They asked me again a couple times after that, but I told them no. I couldn't ever do that again."

"Yet when there's a hanging out in public instead o' inside prison walls, folks bring their babies to watch," Longarm said. "That always strikes me as a damned ugly thing t' do to a kid. But then maybe the idea is to scare them so bad they won't never do nothing so awful that they might end up hanged themselves."

"Then I hope it works, but I'd sure never take a kid of mine to see such a thing," the stationmaster said with considerable feeling. He glanced down at the piles of paper stacked here and there across the surface of his desk. "Can you check back with me later this evening, Marshal? Better yet, late tonight. My men from that shift will be coming on duty at midnight. I'll ask them as they come to clock in."

"All right. I appreciate your help."

"I just hope I can be of service."

"Excuse me now, please. I got some more inquiries t' make around town."

The stationmaster—Longarm had never quite gotten his name—stood and reached across his desk to give Longarm's hand a brisk shake. He was buried nose-down in his flood of papers again before Longarm had time to reach the door and step out into the cool evening air.

In Canon City, as in much of Colorado, there was often a chill in the air once the sun went down, even in the dead of summer. There was a little pale sunlight lingering over the mountain peaks to the south, north, and west of Canon, but already the day's heat was being replaced by a welcome coolness.

In windows and doorways along the streets of the town, lamplight began to show yellow in the dusk.

Most of the traffic in town was pedestrian at this hour. The drays and heavy wagons of commerce had mostly been unhitched and put away for the night, and the workingmen were heading off to supper or a favorite saloon. It was an hour when respectable women would not be seen in public. But the other kind very well might be. A few saddle horses clopped briskly toward whatever amusements their riders had in mind for the evening. It was a pleasant time of day, and Longarm enjoyed the brief walk from the railroad depot over to Old Max.

"Halt!" an unseen guard barked from the shadows at Longarm's approach. "State your business."

Longarm announced himself and added, "Here t' see Warden France."

"Does the warden know you, sir?" The guard still had not shown himself. Smart, Longarm thought.

"He does."

"Wait here." An oblong of dim light showed briefly, silhouetting a man's figure—a man carrying a shotgun, it seemed—then disappeared again with the sound of a door being closed and bolted.

Longarm took out a cheroot and lighted it. He was halfway finished smoking it when the door opened again. This time, two men could be seen moving into the sentry box beside the huge, steel gate.

By then, it was almost fully dark. One of the men displayed a bull's-eye lantern and opened the light portal in front of the reflectors, shining the focused light onto Longarm.

"Long." Longarm thought he could hear a smile in Ned France's voice. "What brings you here to interrupt my supper?"

"I'm sorry, Ned. I never thought about the time."

"Not a social call, eh?"

"No, I'm afraid not."

"Come inside then. Tommy, open the gate for the marshal." To Longarm, he said, "You can come over to my quarters. We can talk about your business while you join me for supper."

Longarm grinned. "That's the best invite I've heard all day, Ned. Thanks."

Cables creaked as the portcullis-style gate was lifted out of the way and a set of heavy, iron-reinforced, oak doors was swung open. It would be just as hard to break into Old Max, Longarm thought, as to break out, and at night it was as much a fortress as a prison.

"How does roast squab sound, Longarm? With fresh peas and new potatoes in garlic butter, then some Napoleon brandy to settle the stomach after. We can talk over the brandy. Unless, that is, your mission is urgent. You know I will be happy to leave my meal if you need me."

"Later will be fine, Ned. Before I forget, though, that young fellow on gate duty right now. Tommy, I b'lieve you call him?"

"Yes?"

"He's good. He don't know me from Adam's off ox, o' course, an' he handled me just fine, a stranger comin' here at this hour and wantin' in."

"That is good to hear, Longarm. I'll pass the compliment along. And put a note in his personnel file too. This way now." The warden tipped his head back and inhaled deeply. "Can you smell it? Ah! Those spices give such a fine aroma."

Longarm couldn't smell a damn thing, but he did not want to ruin Ned's pleasure by saying so. The warden was a man who did thoroughly enjoy his groceries.

"Smells wonderful," Longarm said as he allowed Ned to lead him inside his quarters.

# Chapter 29

"The only man we've discharged in the past week," the warden said once the brandy was poured and cigars lighted, "is Junius Adamson. He was in for counterfeiting."

"Counterfeiting?" Longarm said. "That's a federal offense, Ned. What the devil was the man doing here in a state prison for that?"

France inhaled the aroma rising from his brandy, smiled, and tried a very small sip. The smile expanded as he rolled the liquor over his tongue to fully enjoy the flavor. Then he said, "The man is not the greenest pea in the pod, Longarm. In fact, he's as dumb as a post, near about. He was convicted of printing bogus ten-dollar notes. *Territorial* bank notes!"

"But Colorado hasn't issued its own currency since . . . I don't know when exactly. It was before I came out here, I do know that."

The warden chuckled and nodded. "This was all the way back during the war, Longarm. Adamson was a Confederate sympathizer. He claimed he wanted to raise money for The Cause. His lawyer also claimed he should be exempt from prosecution because what he did was an act of war. The judge didn't buy that. He found Junius guilty of the charges and sentenced him to thirty months in the territorial prison."

"But if he was sent up for two an' a half years, what the hell was he still doin' here this week?" Longarm asked.

"I did mention that Adamson is a stupid son of a bitch, didn't I? Being behind bars didn't make him any smarter. Several times, he attacked guards. He brutalized fellow prisoners. Three times, he was convicted of failed escape attempts." France shrugged. "He kept doing dumb things that resulted in his sentence being extended."

Longarm shook his head. "Idiot," he observed.

"I cannot argue the point," France agreed. "Do you think there is any chance your man could have come here to meet Junius?"

"Hell, Ned, I dunno. Did he have much contact with the outside world while he was in here?"

"None that I am aware of. I know for a fact he never had a visitor the whole time he was with us, and the prison chaplain mentioned once that he never received any mail. Of course, I wouldn't necessarily know about these things. My work is basically administrative. I don't have much direct contact with the inmates. Do you want me to ask my people?"

"No need to make a big thing of it, I think, but if you happen t' think of it when you're talkin' with your officers, it couldn't hurt to ask them. If they connect this Adamson with either Karl Hix or Blake Richards, I'd sure want to know it. Otherwise, don't worry about it, Ned."

The warden nodded. "All right. I'll ask. If nothing comes of it, I'll let it drop there."

Longarm took a gulp of the fiery brandy. He supposed this was good stuff—Ned always liked the best—but brandy was not among his favorite beverages. Too fruity for his taste. But the cigar was good. He wondered how soon he could politely excuse himself so he could go get a shot or two of rye to settle that good meal.

● ● ●

"Par'n me," Longarm said, "but I didn't catch your name this afternoon."

"Ransom Peete," the stationmaster said. "Rance for short."

"Rance it will be then," Longarm said, extending his hand and giving an invitation to use his own nickname. Longarm settled onto one of the straight-backed chairs in Peete's office. He crossed his legs and set his Stetson on his lap. "Have you had a chance t' talk with your people about my fugitives?"

"I did," Peete said. "There is one man I haven't spoken with yet, but none of the others has seen anyone remotely resembling the two you told me about."

"No hoboes ridin' the rods at all lately?"

"Oh, of course there have been some. There most always are. But none that sound like the men you described. I did ask, Longarm, but there have been only a few lately and according to my men, these had long beards and long hair and were pretty old. Older than I understood your fugitives to be."

"Old guys riding the rods?" Longarm said.

"We get a good many of them in their sixties and seventies," Peete explained. "They are too old to work. They have no homes or family, no money. So they go from place to place along the rails and panhandle on the street or beg from door to door. A lot of them were soldiers once. I feel bad for them, but what can I do? It isn't safe for them to ride the rods. It isn't legal either.

"The ones who are really bad off I prosecute," Peete said. "That at least gives them a bed and some decent food for a few days."

Longarm grunted. "Damn if I knew."

"You might be surprised." Peete stood and reached for his coat. "Please excuse me, Longarm. It's been a very long day, and I want to go home to my supper. The only

125

reason I stayed this late was knowing you would be by to get that information. I wish I could have told you something helpful."

Longarm glanced toward the Regulator clock on the wall. It was well past midnight and the stationmaster said he had not yet been home to eat. "I'm sorry t' put you out like that, Rance. Thanks for all your trouble."

"I just wish I could have helped. In the morning, I will ask that last man. If he knows anything about your people, where can I reach you to tell you about it?"

"Damn if I know, Rance. I haven't got around t' findin' a room yet. I'll come by some time tomorra morning anyway, just t' check in with you. Is that all right?"

"Of course." Peete put on his coat and carefully buttoned it, then reached for his hat. He gave Longarm time to get out the door ahead of him, then blew out the lamps and followed, locking the door behind him. "Tomorrow," he said, offering his hand to shake before he walked off into the night, leaving Longarm alone on the dimly lighted depot platform.

# Chapter 30

Longarm was disgusted. There were three hotels in town.
Two had signs out saying they were full. The third was
locked up tight as a nun's pussy and no one came to answer
the bellpull. There were probably boardinghouses in town
too, but he did not know where they might be.

And he was tired, dammit. It had been a long day and he
was feeling more than a little grumpy, all the more so since
his saddle and carpetbag were God knows where in that caboose. Or had been the last time he saw them. By now, he
supposed they could be lying on a trash heap somewhere
up the line.

There was nothing there that could not be replaced, of
course. But it would be a pain in the ass if he had to do it.
Besides, he purely hated shopping.

Disgust at losing track of Hix, annoyance at losing his
gear, and simple fatigue combined to affect both his body
and his mood. His feet hurt and there was a sharp, stabbing
pain high on his back between his shoulder blades, and he
thought he was commencing to get a headache too.

And he did not have a bed to sleep in.

"Shit!" he grumbled aloud. Did not feel any better for it,
though.

He spotted a glow of lamplight close to the railroad depot. A café, he saw when he came closer. Finally, something was going his way. He picked up his pace and limped the last few feet to the door.

Inside, the café smelled of hot lard, coal smoke, and stale sweat. The place was tiny. There were no tables, chairs, or even stools to sit on. A chest-high counter ran along the walls. Piles of cups were strategically placed so anyone who bellied up to the counter could reach them, as were baskets of yeast rolls. There were also bottles of vinegar spaced here and there along the counter, some of them with hot peppers inside.

A little bell jangled whenever the door was opened. It rang to announce Longarm's arrival. There was no one else in the place, at least not in the front. After a few minutes, an enormously fat woman wearing overalls and a grease-stained apron came waddling out. She looked like someone had taken an ordinary woman, poked a hollow straw in her, and inflated her to see how far human skin could be stretched. Pretty damn far to judge by this example. She barely fit through the doorway, and he could not begin to count the number of chins that rippled and wobbled where her throat ought to be.

"Evenin'," Longarm said, taking his hat off. Just because the woman was repulsive did not mean he had to be rude to her.

"Morning is more like it," she said. She had a nice voice. Friendly. And her smile was positively angelic. She cocked her head to one side and eyed him closely. "You don't fit," she declared.

Longarm blinked. "Par'n me?"

"You don't fit. I mean, you don't fit with the customers I generally get here. You certainly aren't train crew, and there has not been a passenger car stop here for hours. Sometimes, we get passengers off the stagecoach if their schedule is off, like if they have to change a wheel or break an axle, but the stage came by right on time already this evening. So I have to wonder where a fine gentleman like you fits."

Just because she was fat, Longarm was reminded, it did not necessarily follow that she was stupid too. And she had that great smile. He liked her. He smiled—the first time he had felt like doing that lately—and introduced himself and explained his situation.

The woman clucked sympathetically. "Lost all your things, you say, in Tommy Hart's caboose? My, oh, my. That is . . . that is funny, that's what that is."

"Not from my point o' view, it ain't," Longarm protested.

"Don't worry about it, dearie. I know every fellow that works on this line. They all come eat here. I'll tell you what. I will have one of the boys send a message . . . service traffic, you won't have to pay anything for the telegram . . . up the line. They'll find your things and route them back here to you. How does that sound?"

"You can do that?"

"I said I could, didn't I?"

"You," he said, "are an angel."

Her smile became even bigger, although he would not have thought that possible. "Anything for a friend," she said, ignoring the fact that they just now met.

"May I ask you a personal question?" he said.

"If it isn't too, too personal, dearie. If you know what I mean." She batted her eyelashes at him and laughed.

"What I was wantin' to know," he said, "is your name."

"Didn't I . . . oh! I suppose I didn't." She curtsied. Rather nicely too. "Sallie Queen is my name. It's my real name too, not something made up. Everybody calls me Queenie. Ask anywhere up and down the line, they all know Queenie."

"And a pleasure it is to meet you, Queenie."

"Likewise. Listen, dearie, are you hungry? We only serve one meal. That's stew. It's good stew too if I do say so. Nice and thick. It will put hair on your chest."

"Thanks, but I came in hoping to find a cup of coffee and a chair to sit in. My feet hurt something awful."

Sallie glanced over her shoulder at the big railroad-quality Regulator on the wall. "I tell you what. There isn't another train due through for more than an hour and there won't be a crew change made on it. At the most, I might get some deadheaders coming in for breakfast, but that won't be for a while. If you promise you won't tell anyone, I can bring my stool out and let you use that to rest on. That and a cup of coffee maybe?"

"That sounds wonderful, Sallie."

The fat woman disappeared into the back of the place, and emerged a moment later carrying a tall kitchen stool. She set it down, then went back and brought out a steaming coffeepot. "This is a little old, but it will do the trick."

She took a cup off the nearest stack, turned it rightside-up, and poured it full, sliding it in front of Longarm. "This will get your pecker up."

Longarm gaped, not entirely sure he'd heard that correctly.

Queenie roared with laughter. "It's something Englishmen say, dearie, not what you think. It means keep your head up. Your lips. A little kiss is a peck, right?" She laughed again. "Nope, not what you thought I said, not at all."

"You aren't English," he protested.

"No, but I think the expression is funny."

Longarm just shook his head.

Queenie removed her apron, wadded it up into a loose ball, and tossed it onto the counter. "Can I trust you in here, Deputy Marshal Long? Will you promise not to steal all my valuable paintings if I leave you alone in here for a few minutes?"

He looked slowly around at the walls, which were bare except for two signs. One simply had a large, bright red "25" drawn on it—cents, he assumed, for the bread, stew, and coffee that constituted a meal here—and the other read, "No spitting on floor." Valuable paintings indeed. "I think I can restrain myself," he said dryly.

"I'll be right back," Queenie said. She waddled out into the night.

Longarm perched on the stool and sighed, pleased to be able to stretch his feet out and wiggle his toes. It would have been even better had he been able to take his boots off.

He tried the coffee. It was stout as a Missouri mule, but it tasted good. All the better he got a cigar lighted. No spitting on the floor, but what about spent matches and the like? He looked around, but there were no ashtrays in evidence. He settled for placing the blackened match stem and flake of tobacco he had removed from the end twist onto the edge of the counter, intending to ask Queenie where he should dispose of them when she returned.

She was back before he was finished with the coffee. The first thing she did was to retrieve her apron and put it on. Then she said, "I've sent that message. Your things should show up here tomorrow morning sometime."

"Really?"

"I said it, didn't I?"

"Thank you, Queenie. You're a jewel."

"You are right. I am. No one but you and I seem to know that, though," she said, then laughed. Queenie's laugh was as bright and friendly as her smile.

Longarm drained the last of his coffee and set the cup down with a sigh. He reluctantly got off the stool, his feet hurting anew once he did so. "Reckon I'd best go find a spot t' stretch out. On a bench over to the depot, more'n likely. There doesn't seem to be anything open where a fellow can find a room at this hour."

"I have a thought about that too," Queenie said. "If you aren't too fastidious."

"A pile o' straw would be good enough if there ain't too much manure in it," he answered.

"No manure, but I haven't changed the sheets in a couple days."

"What . . . ?"

"Obviously, I am not using my bed, and I won't be getting off from work here until past dawn. I have a little shack about five blocks from here. You would be welcome to use it tonight."

"That is might' nice o' you, Queenie."

"Does that mean you accept?"

"Yes. Absolutely. Thank you."

She fished underneath her apron, obviously in a pocket there, and after a moment brought a key out. She handed him the key and gave him detailed directions about how to find her "little shack," which in fact turned out to be a modest but very nice—and impeccably clean—bungalow.

Once there, Longarm stripped off his clothes—he felt like he had been wearing them continuously for the past month—and dropped onto Queenie's feather bed.

# Chapter 31

Longarm groaned. His head felt hollow, and he had no sense of where his arms or his legs were. They were weightless. Lost. He felt as if he were floating in a warm pool.

This feeling of near-sleep would have been perfect except for one lone annoyance. It took him a few moments to sort out the sensations and identify the one thing that kept this from being perfect. There was daylight from a newly rising sun streaming in and bothering him.

Logically, he should get up and pull the curtains closed. Yep. That is what he should do, all right.

Fuck it!

He rolled over onto his side and dragged a pillow over his eyes, then allowed himself a gentle and dreamy drift back into sleep.

Sometime later—it could have been only minutes, but felt like it must have been several hours at least—he came half awake again.

He felt . . . he had a hard-on actually. His cock was stiff and eager.

And warm.

He felt like he was engulfed in warmth. Wet and gently insistent. He felt . . . be damned. What he felt like was that his dick was inside a pussy. Except he was alone in this deep, soft feather bed.

Wasn't he?

Longarm stiffened. The rest of him did, that is. His cock was already stiff as a tent pole.

He felt a slight shift of weight on the soft mattress— someone else's weight; he had not moved—and a warm, wet tug on his pecker.

He heard a moist, slurping sound and then a sigh.

Chill morning air on wet flesh magnified the coldness when his cock was released from wherever it had been.

For one ugly moment, the thought flashed into his mind that somehow Joe Templeton's queer son had caught up with him, and . . . his erection sagged and he reached for the pillow over his eyes so he could see who was there.

Then he heard a woman's voice whisper, "Lie still. Let me do this. Please."

Longarm grunted. He left the pillow where it was.

He could feel the woman's breath warm on the head of his cock, and his erection surged back hard and strong.

He felt the tip of her tongue drag teasingly up and down the length of his shaft. Then down onto his balls.

Strong hands tugged his legs apart, and the dancing tongue moved to the underside of his balls and then briefly onto his asshole.

"No," he mumbled. "Not . . . there."

Obligingly, the tongue returned to his balls. Gently, one at a time, he felt them being drawn into the mouth, then again released. The tongue resumed its travel onto his cock. It made the long journey to the bulbous head and rimmed the opening there. It burrowed underneath his foreskin and moved around and around.

He became impatient for more, his hips thrusting slightly although he was barely aware of the motion.

His bedmate must have felt the movement and sensed the reason for it, because she withdrew her probing tongue and again took Longarm's cock into the moist cavity of her mouth.

She suckled there as if seeking milk from a tit.

Soon—it could have been seconds or long minutes later; time had absolutely no meaning for him right then—he felt the hot, sweet rise of sap deep within his balls.

He began to tremble. Tried to hold it back.

It was no use. His jism shot hard into her mouth. Pumped and kept on flowing, the feeling intense and continuous.

When finally the flow was exhausted, his body went limp, sated now and totally relaxed.

He thought about getting up. Or at least moving the pillow so he could see his bedmate. See who the hell she was anyway.

But a soft whisper urged, "Sleep now, dearie. Sleep well."

That was the last he remembered.

# Chapter 32

He woke—the next time—to the aroma of coffee and the sound of something sizzling in a frying pan.

Longarm sat up and yawned. He rubbed his eyes and looked around the interior of Queenie's house. She was standing at the stove with a spatula in hand and a smile on her round face. "Good morning. Or should I say good afternoon."

"God. It isn't. Is it?"

She laughed."Yes, it is, as a matter of fact. I was beginning to think you were going to sleep another night through."

"What, uh, time 'zit?"

"Late. Afternoon sometime. I'm not sure." She set the spatula down and went to the windows, pulling the drapes open one by one until daylight flooded the room.

"I'm sorry. I've taken up your bed, an' you worked all night. You must be sleepy."

"I'm fine. I slept in my chair." She inclined her head in the direction of a stout, deeply upholstered armchair and footstool. A knitted afghan lay draped over the back of the oversized chair. "Don't think you chased me. Sometimes I sleep in that chair anyhow. It seems to help the aches and pains in my back."

He almost asked if that had indeed been her who joined him in the bed earlier, but that would have been a damned rude thing to discuss. And it was not important anyway. It had been good. And mighty relaxing. Whatever and whoever, he for one had no regrets. Instead, he said, "What're you cookin' there?"

"Ham. Potatoes. I got some eggs in the bowl ready to go in the grease as soon as these come out. Are you hungry?"

"Does a bear . . . oh . . . uh, never mind."

Queenie laughed. "I know. Does a bear shit in the woods. I don't think, dearie, you are going to say anything that I haven't heard before."

"Dearie." The woman with the marvelous mouth and tongue had called him that. So it almost had to be Queenie who visited him. Almost.

"I'm starved," he said, swinging his legs off the side of the bed.

"The thunder mug is in that commode over there," Queenie offered.

"You got an outhouse? I ain't in so much of a hurry that I got to dirty your crock."

"Yes, but you'd best put some clothes on before you go outside. I do have neighbors, you know. They might object to having a naked man prowling around in my backyard."

He looked down. He had quite forgotten that one little fact. "Oops. Sorry."

"Oh, it is all right with me. I told you it is the neighbors who might find fault." She chuckled and returned her attention to the sizzling spuds and ham in her skillet.

Longarm quickly pulled his clothes on and stepped outside barefoot, picking his way carefully across the yard to the backhouse, where he took his time about doing his business. When he returned to the house, there was a basin, a pitcher of clean water, and a fresh towel laid out on a small table that hadn't been there when he left. Queenie appeared in the doorway a moment later with a dish of runny soap.

"After you eat," she said, "I'll give you a bath."

"Oh, that ain't nec . . ."

"I'd like to. If you don't mind." She sounded suddenly shy.

"I'd like it too," he lied.

He washed, splashed the cool water onto his face, and wondered if he could find a barber still open. He needed a shave.

Queenie had prepared a mountain of food, and did more than her share of making it disappear. She was a good cook, though. The spuds were fried brown and just crisp enough to be tasty, the ham slightly crusty too, and the eggs were served sunny-side up with plenty of salt and a little pepper. She also produced a pan of biscuits from the oven and made red-eye ham gravy to pour over them. Longarm had had worse meals.

When finally he pushed back from the table, she picked up a bucket and headed out to the pump in the backyard.

Longarm hurried to take the pail from her, and carried bucket after bucket of icy cold water inside until her slipper tub, which she stored upright in a closet, was half full. Meanwhile, Queenie was heating a kettle of water to take the chill off his bath.

"In you go," she said when she was satisfied with both the depth and the temperature of the bathwater.

"Are you sure you . . ."

"In!" she ordered.

Longarm shucked out of his clothing and stepped into the tub.

Queenie, looking quite pleased with the opportunity, fetched a washrag and her little tub of soft soap.

"Now be quiet and let me enjoy myself," she said.

Longarm did as she asked.

• • •

"What time 'zit?" Longarm asked sleepily. He was standing on a braided rug, warm and feeling mighty good while Queenie worked him over with a huge, fluffy towel.

"Along about dark," she told him.

"Late," he said.

"I'm afraid so. I hate to say it as I'm having such a pleasant time, but as soon as I finish drying you, dearie, I have to change clothes and go to work. I'm afraid I will be late as it is."

"Shit! I don't mean t' get you in trouble."

"You won't. I'm about the only one fool enough to work all night there by myself. Old Henry wouldn't dare fire me." She giggled. "Besides, half the railroaders on the line would give him hell if he tried. But I don't want to be any later than I have to."

"Go along then. I can take over from here."

"But I . . ."

"Honest, Queenie. I been dressin' myself for, oh, quite a few years now. Reckon I can manage on my own again now."

"All right. But I really have been having fun. Thank you, dearie." She hurried behind a privacy screen, and emerged a minute or so later wearing a work dress and clean apron, a grotesquely fat but nonetheless sweet little woman.

"Let yourself out when you're ready, or stay the night again if you like," she said as she picked up her bonnet and handbag.

"Thanks but I'd best be moving along. I got t' check back with the warden an' the stationmaster about my boys."

"I can ask after them too if you like," she offered.

"If you think to. That would be a big help," he said.

"Is there anything else . . . ?"

"Go on now. I don't wanta be responsible for you gettin'

140

in trouble with your boss. And Queenie . . . Sallie . . . thanks. For everything."

Longarm was not sure, but he thought Queenie was blushing when she stepped outside and hurried away in the dusk of early evening.

# Chapter 33

Longarm walked over to the railroad depot first, but the stationmaster's office was closed. Two porters were outside on the platform rolling dice on the bed of an empty luggage cart, and inside the building a young man sat behind the ticket window reading a newspaper. Longarm ambled over to the window.

"Where to, mister?"

"I'm here looking for Mr. Peete."

The clerk shook his head. "Gone for the night. He'll be back here about seven thirty."

"What time is it now?" Longarm turned around, looking for a clock—there are always clocks in view in a railroad station—but the clerk said, "In the morning, mister."

"Damn!"

The young man grinned. "Not to my way of looking at it. He don't . . . excuse me, doesn't . . . Mr. Peete doesn't allow us to read anything but timetables and rate schedules when we're on railroad time."

"Go back to your newspaper then, son."

The young clerk winked and let the pages of the *Canon City Record* drop aside, revealing the magazine he had been hiding there. It was one of the more luridly imaginative of the dime novels. Longarm could not see the title—and did not particularly want to—but the portion of the cover illustration that he did see was enough to tell him what sort of tale it offered.

"I stand corrected. Go back to your educational material there."

"Yes, sir," the clerk said happily. "This one is about Big Foot Wallace and the Nez Perce. It's good."

Big Foot Wallace had been a real person, but he was part of Texas border lore and likely never heard of the Nez Percé tribe. Which the youngster had mispronounced.

Longarm turned away, chuckling softly, and headed for the door. The clerk had his nose buried in his dime novel again before Longarm had gone two steps.

He went out onto the platform—the two Negro porters were gone now—and stopped there to search in his coat for a cheroot and a match. He still had a few matches, but no more cigars.

Oh, he'd brought a good supply along for this trip. But they were all in his luggage, dammit.

Annoyed, he left the depot and headed for the business district that ran parallel to the railroad a block north of the tracks. The prison, where he needed to go anyway to see Ned France again in case the warden had heard something about Richards and Hix, was at the west end of the six-block-long business district, so he had to go more or less in that direction anyway.

"Shit!" Longarm stopped in the middle of the street and muttered aloud.

The only lights showing at this hour were in a few saloons. Every store in sight was closed up tight as a virgin's ass. Every damned one. He changed direction and entered the nearest saloon.

"Evenin', mister," the barkeep greeted. "Beer?"

Longarm thought about Ned France and his fruity brandy. "Whiskey," he said. "And d'you offer cigars?"

"I got some crooks here," the bartender said as he deftly took a tin mug down from a pile of them stacked pyramid-like, ready for the night's traffic. "The first one comes free with your whiskey. If you want more'n that, I got to charge you for them."

"I'll take a dozen then."

"You understand I got to charge you." The man splashed a generous tot of liquor into the mug.

Judging from the pale color, Longarm guessed the "whiskey" here was homemade, probably a mixture of grain alcohol and whatever else was handy when the blend was put together. Some of the worst whiskey Longarm ever tasted was that rough-and-ready sort. And some of it wasn't half bad.

"That's fine."

The barkeep set the mug in front of Longarm and turned away saying, "I'll get those cigars for you."

Longarm took a very small and tentative sip of the liquor. His eyebrows went up and he began to smile. He dropped his chin and positioned his nose over the mug so he could take in the aroma. Then he tried another sip. And then a swallow. Damn but this stuff was *good*.

"Meet your approval, mister?" the barkeep said. He laid a dozen pale cigars onto the bar counter beside Longarm's whiskey.

"Damn, I reckon. That's good stuff."

The barman chuckled. "I make it myself. Secret recipe, though, so don't ask. Try one of these cigars, friend. I told you, the first one is free. If you don't like it, you don't have to buy the others."

"I got t' tell you," Longarm said, "I'm glad I stopped in here tonight." He drained the mug and smacked his lips. "Let's do that again, shall we?"

It was late before Longarm presented himself at the Old Max gate. And he was not quite as steady on his feet as he might have been.

145

# Chapter 34

"Are you Mr. Long?" the gate guard asked.

"I am Deputy United States Marshal Custis Long, I shall have you know," Longarm announced, rather more loudly than he intended. He swayed a little to one side, righted himself with a grab for the gate, leaned the other way, then brought himself back to center. "Yes," he said. "I am."

"The warden said if you was to show up here, we was to bring you to his quarters, mister."

"Marshal," Longarm corrected. "Deppity marshal."

"Yeah, whatever. D'you wanna come with me? D'you need help?"

"I can walk by myself, young man." That was, however, at least somewhat in doubt, and he did not offer any objections when the guard took him by the arm to help steady him. The guard led him inside and across the prison yard to the little stone house provided for the warden's use.

There were no lights showing inside until the guard rapped on the door. Then there was a short wait and a light bobbed closer, the motion making it plain that the lamp or candle was being carried from the back of the place.

When he opened the door, Ned France was in a dressing gown and carpet slippers. It was later than Longarm had realized.

"Longarm. There you are." He looked past Longarm's shoulder to his guard. "Thank you, Jimmy."

"Did you still . . . ?"

"You did right, Jimmy. Thanks for bringing him."

"Yes, sir. Excuse me now. I got to get back to my post."

France took Longarm by the sleeve and pulled him inside. Once there, he held a lighted hurricane lamp high and peered closely at his friend's face. "Longarm, you are drunk."

"I am not," Longarm protested. "But I may be a wee bit tipsy."

"Then I suggest you sober up in a hurry. Your boss has had messages out all over this part of the country, looking for you."

Longarm blinked. And stood up straighter, the effects of his evening of drinking sloughing away in the face of duty. "What's wrong?" His voice was steady when he asked it.

"I don't know but Mr. Peete, the stationmaster down the street, came by here looking for you. He said he has at least two messages there for you but he didn't want to acknowledge that you were here until you said it was all right. Just in case, well, you know."

Longarm took a deep breath, held it for a moment, then slowly exhaled. "Thanks, Ned. I was just over there. He . . . come to think of it, it's been a while now. Messages, you say? That would mean the telegrapher on duty should have them for me even if Rance isn't there at this hour. What the hell time is it anyway?"

"Somewhere around two in the morning," Ned told him.

"Time sure does fly when you're havin' fun, don't it," Longarm said, shaking his head. "Sorry I bothered you."

"No bother." The warden smiled and added, "But don't make a habit of it."

Longarm apologized again, then headed back toward the gate. He needed to get back to the railroad depot and ask for those messages.

# Chapter 35

"What time did these come in?" Longarm asked as he carefully folded the yellow flimsies and tucked them away inside his coat.

"The first one, that one there just asking you your whereabouts, came in at . . . let me see." The telegrapher rummaged on his desk for his copy of the message forms and adjusted his spectacles higher on his nose before he spoke again. "That first one was received at 1043, Marshal. That is the time I receipted for it, not when it started coming across the wire. The second one"—he shuffled the papers to find the second message—"the one telling you about the robbery, that one came in at 1312. That would be twelve minutes past one to you civilians, sir."

"Thank you," Longarm said, biting back an impulse to snarl at the young man for assuming he would not know how to tell time from the twenty-four-hour clock used by telegraphers. And soldiers.

He was feeling more than a little peevish right now, but it had nothing to do with this helpful telegraph operator. He was pissed off at himself for being out of touch like he had been all day long.

It was one thing to be unavailable because he was busy in the pursuit of his duties. It was quite another to be side-tracked for the sake of a blow job and some booze.

He sighed. Not that he would have been able to do anything to save that poor sonuvabitch postal clerk Billy Vail's wires reported on.

Billy's first wire was asking any available deputy in the vicinity to respond to a reported robbery in Wetmore.

The second added that the post office clerk there had been gunned down in the commission of that robbery.

Unlike Longarm's personal vendetta against Joe Templeton's murderer, which really was a state case so far as law enforcement was concerned, this was a federal offense and his responsibility.

"I want you t' send a response t' this," Longarm told the telegrapher, tapping his coat where the message forms were.

"At this hour, sir? Surely, the marshal's office won't be open at this hour."

"No, but the marshal will get it first thing when he gets t' work in a few hours."

"Oh. Well . . . yes, I suppose he would."

"Trust me, son. He will."

"What do you want to say, sir?"

"Just send, 'Long en route Wetmore.' That should be enough."

"Just those words, sir? Don't you want to sign it or anything?"

"Just those words. That tells him everything he needs t' know."

"Yes, sir."

"There is somethin' else you can do for me, though," Longarm told the night telegraph operator.

"If I can."

"I need t' get down there to this Wetmore place. I've heard the name. Supposed t' be a mining community somewhere down in the Wet Mountains, but I don't exactly know where 'tis. Nor how t' get there. I'm hopin' maybe you can help me out on that score."

"Of course." The young man tore a message form off a pad on his desk and picked up a pencil. "I'm not much good at drawing maps, but I can give you a general idea of where you're going." He put the tip of his pencil on the paper and said, "This is us here in Canon City. Now down along this way is Florence, right along the railroad tracks. See there?"

"I know where Florence is, o' course."

"Now from Florence, see . . ."

# Chapter 36

"There won't be an eastbound passenger train for about another six and a half hours, Marshal," the telegraph operator said.

"It don't have t' be a passenger. When is there a freight comin' through?"

The telegrapher turned to examine the big Regulator mounted on the wall, then calculated the difference between the current time and the scheduled arrival. "About twenty-three minutes, sir. If he's on time, which he usually is. But it's a through freight going on to Pueblo. It won't be stopping here."

"Yes, it will," Longarm said. "Here and in Florence too."

"Oh, I don't know about tha—"

"Official business," Longarm snapped. "Now go lay your torpedoes an' put up the stop signal. I figure t' be on that train."

The clerk hesitated for only a moment until the hard set of Longarm's expression warned him that this would not be a good time to cite railroad regulations. If the federal officer insisted that the train be stopped, then it damn sure was going to stop.

"Yes, sir," he said.

The clerk hurried out into the night, leaving his key unattended for the moment, to do whatever it was he had to do to bring that freight train to an unscheduled halt.

Longarm sat wearily down on a bench in the waiting area. It was almost three o'clock in the morning now and his evening of drinking was catching up with him. "Dammit," he mumbled to himself, "I ain't quite as young as I used t' be." He reached inside his coat for a cigar, trimmed the twist off the tip, and thumbed a match out of his vest pocket. The cigar could not compare with his favorite cheroots or one of the expensive Hernandez y Hernandez panatelas, but it wasn't bad.

He barely had time to smoke it before a series of short whistles announced the impending arrival of the eastbound. The telegraph operator poked his head into the waiting area moments later. "Ready, Marshal?"

"You bet." He was on his feet and out the door practically before the telegrapher could get out of the way.

"Did my key sound while I was out?" the young man asked.

"Not a peep," Longarm told him.

"Thank goodness. I don't want to get in trouble."

"If anyone complains, tell them to see me. Like I said, this here is official business of the United States gummint."

"Yes, sir. Now when the train comes to a stop, you'll want to climb up in the cab with the engineer and the fireman, sir. You said it's Florence you need to get to?"

"That's right."

"Well, there is no stop scheduled for there either. The engineer might not want to stop there."

"Oh, I can pretty much promise you that he'll stop. But just t' be on the safe side with other traffic, you might wanta wire ahead for the Florence station t' put out their stop signal too. Can you do that for me, please?"

"Yes, sir, I will."

"Thank you, son. I appreciate your help."

The eastbound, pulling a coaler, nine open cars of ore, and a caboose, came to a grinding, clanking, hissing halt just past the passenger platform. As soon as the wheels stopped turning, the engineer stuck his head out the window and shouted, "What's wrong? Trouble ahead?"

The telegrapher pointed to Longarm, then disappeared back inside his work station.

Longarm hurried across the platform and began scrambling up the steel ladder onto the tall, powerful engine.

"Who the hell are you and what do you think you're doing getting onto my engine?" the gray-haired man demanded.

Longarm reached inside his coat for the wallet that held his badge. "Let's go, friend. You got a schedule t' keep."

# Chapter 37

The eastbound had slowed to a walking pace when Longarm dropped off the ladder at the Florence platform. Immediately, the engineer, whose name was Brandywine and who had three daughters, two of them still unmarried—damn, Longarm was happy to get off that train—poured the steam to the locomotive and the train began extending to the full length permitted by the couplings. Steel clashed on steel as each coupling took the weight of the cars behind it.

Longarm stood clear as the cars slowly built speed. He was about to turn away when he heard someone shout. It was the same brakeman he had seen on the westbound mixed freight out of Pueblo earlier.

"Hey, mister? Did you get your saddle and carpetbag?"

"No! Where the hell are they?" Longarm shouted, trotting along the platform now to keep pace with the open boxcar where the brakeman was standing on a ladder.

"Pueblo, mister. I sent them on to Pueblo."

Great. Just great. But at least he knew where they were. "All right, thanks," he shouted to the quickly receding form of the brakeman. Longarm slowed his pace and halted.

It was sometime after four in the morning and Longarm found himself standing on an empty platform. A yellow glow of lamplight shined from a small window set high on the side wall of the Florence depot. Longarm headed in that direction.

"You're Long?" the night telegrapher asked when Longarm let himself into the shack.

"That's right. How did you know that?"

The telegrapher, a thin man with one leg, looked at him like he thought Longarm was none too bright.

"Oh. O' course. The Canon City operator gave you my name when he told you I was comin'."

"That's right, but I don't know why you're here. Been no trouble around here. Hell, man, nothin' ever happens 'round here. Never."

"I need to get to the post office in Wetmore," Longarm said, "an' I'm in a hurry."

"Shit, everybody's in a hurry, alla damn time. Tell me somethin' I don't know already."

"Where can I rent a horse?" Longarm asked.

"Canon City. They got a livery stable in Canon. Ain't none around here, though."

"Then how the fuck is a man supposed to get to Wetmore from here?" he demanded.

The telegrapher shrugged, making it plain that this was not his worry. He turned away, plucked a match out of a box of them on the desk, and used the wooden stem to pick his teeth for a moment before he shrugged again and said, "Take the stage is what I'd recommend."

"There's a stagecoach?"

"I jus' now said there was, didn't I?"

"Yes. Fine. So where can I get this coach down t' Wetmore?"

"If'n it's on schedule, you can pick it up right here."

"When would that be?"

The telegrapher grinned. "Stage'll be along to meet the eastbound passenger. That's due in a little past eleven."

160

"Ah, for cryin' out fucking loud," Longarm complained. "They coulda told me that back in Canon City without me having to stop your through freight."

"Did you ask?"

"No, maybe not. An' before you say anything more, no, I didn't explain what-all I needed once I got here, all right?"

The telegraph operator shrugged again and gave him a smart-ass look.

Longarm sighed. "Where can I get a bite of breakfast while I'm waitin' for that stagecoach t' get here?"

The young man walked over to the doorway and pointed. "You go across the street there and down to the next cross street, see. Then turn left and . . ."

# Chapter 38

By the time the stagecoach deposited Longarm in the tiny settlement of Wetmore, it was well past dark. One thing was damned convenient, he thought as he stepped down from the old mud wagon that served the tiny express company as a passenger, mail, and sometimes freight coach . . . he did not have to worry about hauling his baggage around. Not when all his things were in Pueblo.

He patted his pockets. He had four cigars left and . . . he counted . . . eight loose cartridges in his right-hand pocket. And of course there was the derringer that he carried on one end of his vest chain, the other being attached to his Ingersoll timepiece.

He felt like he needed a bath and he damn sure needed a change of clothes.

He decided against smoking another cigar right now. The inside of his mouth felt like he had fuzz growing there. Green mold maybe. And he needed a shave too.

Still, he had work to do.

The stage had stopped outside a small store. It was open, but not for business. A knot of men stood outside smoking. A gaggle of women were inside chattering. On the counter, a coffin was laid out. Longarm could not see from where he stood at street level, but he assumed the recently departed would have been the postal clerk whose murder had brought him here. He stepped forward and introduced himself to the nearest bunch of washed and Sunday-dressed men.

"Deputy U.S. marshal, you say," one of them responded.

"Yes, sir, that's right."

"You figure to go after the ones that killed Anderson?"

"That was his name, Anderson?"

"Ayuh. Harry Anderson. Decent man. A little tight maybe, but decent."

"What happened? Can any of you tell me that?"

More men were drifting nearer now as snippets of the conversation were overheard, drawing attention to the fact that a federal peace officer had come to see about the murder of one of their own.

"It was late in the afternoon," someone said.

"After most of the day's receipts was in the cash box," another put in. "That was smart of them, I figure."

"There was two. Wilma Hanks was . . . hey, Wilma, come out here . . . Wilma Hanks was in the store. She can tell you. Oh, she was scared half to death, she said. Wilma, get out here for a minute. There's somebody wants to talk to you."

A tall, very handsome woman of middle years came out onto the porch. She had broad shoulders and powerful forearms that suggested she had wrung a lot of laundry in her time, and likely milked a good many cows as well.

Longarm went through his introduction again.

"Yes, I was here when it happened," she told him. "I came to pick up a little saleratus and some thread. I was over there by the box of sewing notions when those two ruffians came in. I took one look at them and knew they were up to no good, let me tell you." She frowned and sniffed loudly.

"What did they look like?" Longarm asked.

164

"I already told you. Ruffians."

"Yes, ma'am, but what were they wearing? How tall were they? Were they dark or fair? Did they have facial hair? Did they show their guns right off? What did they say? I need to know everything you can tell me, ma'am. Please."

"Very well. Let me think." She turned and shouted toward the women inside the store. "Ada, you come out here. You were there when Harry was shot. Help me tell this marshal about it."

Ada Smith was a small, weathered woman who was probably in her twenties but looked fifty.

Between the two women going back and forth at each other, Longarm got what he hoped was a fairly clear account of the robbery.

Two men had entered together and immediately displayed their revolvers. The taller of them was in charge. He ordered Anderson to open his safe—there was no safe, but the storekeeper did have a heavy steel cash box that he kept beneath the counter—and to empty it into a flour sack.

Anderson, the women said, complied with the instructions he was given by the taller robber. The second man stood with his back to the counter, waving his pistol left to right and back again and keeping an eye on the doorway and the two ladies who happened to be in the store at the time.

"That one did not say anything. Not a word the whole time he was in here. It was the other that did all the talking. Well, him and his gun."

Harry Anderson did exactly what he was told. He was nervous and fumbled with the twine when he was ordered to tie the flour sack closed. "So the coins would not fall out, one would presume."

The tall one told Anderson to put his hands up and keep them up, which he did. Then the robber picked up the sack and said, "Come on, Carl, we got it all."

Longarm interrupted. "That's what he said? You're sure? 'Come on Carl'?"

"That is right."

"Exactly right. I can still hear it in my head."

"I can still see what happened after," the other lady said. "I will see that to the end of my days, Marshal. To the end of my days.

"The tall one came out from behind the counter. The other one, this scruffy Carl person, snickered. Oh, it was an evil sound. And he just turned and pointed that big, black pistol at poor Harry, who was standing there with his hands raised—he wasn't moving or trying to get away or anything but what he was told to do. The awful man pointed his pistol in Mr. Anderson's face and just . . . pulled the trigger."

"It was a terrible sound, that gun going off," the other lady said. "Terrible. I can hear it yet."

"Harry, well, I can't tell you what happened to him. It was simply awful what that bullet did to him."

"Yes, ma'am." Longarm did not have to be told something like that. He had seen it for himself. More times than he ever would have wanted to. A large-caliber bullet in the face is just plain damned messy.

"Then the both of them ran outside," the ladies continued. "They grabbed some horses that were tied out there. Not their own horses, we understand. And they just rode away."

"The tall one seemed mad that the scruffy one did what he did. But of course it was too late then to change anything."

Longarm turned to the men who were gathered close around them by now. "What about the horses?" he asked. "Whose were they?"

"They belonged to a couple of men who live down the mountain a little piece. They were in town to have some drinks and visit . . . well . . . you know the sort of thing a man might do."

"Uh-huh."

166

"Those horses, Marshal, I heard they was turned loose. They come back to their home place already."

"And this happened when?"

"Day before yesterday, late in the afternoon."

Longarm grimaced. The horses must not have been ridden too terribly far if they had returned home already.

Just down to the railroad perhaps?

"Tell us, Marshal. Do you want us to get a horse for you so you can track those fellas come first light?"

Longarm shook his head. "No need."

"But . . ."

"I already know where they're going," he told the crowd. "Now if you'll excuse me . . ." Longarm stepped up onto the porch and removed his hat before going inside to pay his respects to the storekeeper and part-time postal clerk who was laid out in the box there.

Then he went outside to ask about the quickest way back down to Florence and the railroad.

# Chapter 39

The penny-ante stagecoach was scheduled to go all the way to Silver Cliff before it turned around for the back-haul, and there was no way Longarm intended to wait for its return. He offered two dollars to anyone who would lend him a horse that would get him back down to the railroad.

"If you ain't too proud to be seen behind a mare, Marshal, I got me a fast trotter and a light buggy will get you there in jig time. And you don't need to be paying me for the use of her neither, though I'll do the driving if you don't mind. She's used to my hand on the lines."

"That's might' kind of you, friend."

"Harry Anderson wasn't what you'd call a friendly man, but he was one of our own. We want his killers caught."

"Then get your rig and I'll get after them," Longarm promised.

He was indeed back in Florence in "jig time." And thanks to Weed Holt's driving, he was even able to get a little sleep doing it.

Holt deposited him back at the Florence depot just short of dawn.

"I need a ride back to Pueblo," Longarm declared when he burst into the stationmaster's office.

"And you are exactly who?" a stout man with more belly than hair demanded.

Longarm introduced himself.

"Oh, you're the one that's been making us interrupt our schedule," the fat man said. "Well, you won't find that so easy to do here. I allow no disruption."

"Is the next outfit through scheduled to stop?"

"It is not. It's a through freight next, then a passenger eastbound later in the morning."

Longarm smiled. "What d'you want to bet you decide t' stop that freight an' put me on it," he said.

"That will not happen, sir."

Longarm took his handcuffs out of his pocket. "Then, mister, you can turn yourself around, because if I *ain't* on that eastbound freight, you are gonna be going with me as my prisoner later on when I can catch the passenger."

"You can't bluff me."

"Mister, I ain't bluffing." Longarm hauled the man off his chair, spun him around, and snapped a cuff onto one wrist. Before he had time to finish the job of applying the bracelets, the gentleman had a change of mind on whether that train could be stopped for a passenger.

# Chapter 40

Longarm dropped off Engine No. 412 in the yard. There was no need for him to stay with the train all the way to the smelter. The spot he wanted was right there close to the train yard anyway.

"Thanks," he said, saluting the engineer with a touch of his hat brim.

"Any time, Marshal. Good luck."

Longarm appreciated the good wishes, never mind that he did not expect these two jaspers to offer a problem. A pair of small-time hoodlums like Blake Richards and Karl Hix were nothing to worry about.

And from the descriptions he got back in Wetmore, those two were the ones that robbed the post office there.

Richards, he figured, would surely have been the one to see an opportunity for the robbery. Longarm did not know if Richards and Hix knew each other in the past or if their acquaintance was a recent thing, but he guessed that Richards needed a man to watch his back while he raked in the goodies.

He made his mistake, though, when he chose Karl Hix as his backup. Hix had been kicked around pretty much his

171

whole life through. Of course, the fact that the man was an asshole contributed heavily to that, but the fact remained.

The problem with Hix as a backup man was that murdering Joe Templeton in cold blood back there in Denver gave the son of a bitch a taste for power and for blood.

He discovered that he *liked* killing a defenseless victim.

To Longarm's mind, that put Karl Hix in much the same category as a mad dog. And all you can do with one of those is to shoot it.

In Hix's case, Longarm figured a hangman's noose would substitute nicely. With two murders on his plate, he was sure to hang. And with two murders behind him, the U.S. attorney was sure to let the State of Colorado try him, the federal government not having the death penalty for ordinary crimes.

If you could call any murder "ordinary."

Longarm pulled out his last cigar, bit the twist off the end, and spat it out, then fished a lucifer out of his vest pocket and snapped it alight with his thumbnail. Now that he was back in civilization, he should be able to get some decent smokes again. That was enough to brighten his day.

He glanced overhead at the position of the sun. It was past noon and his belly was rumbling, reminding him that it had been a while since he last ate. He had gotten a little sleep on the ride down from Wetmore to Florence, but had not thought to grab a meal there too. Now he regretted that oversight.

There was no sense wasting time on food, though. If he could catch the two robbers lying abed after a night of indulgence, all the better. He turned and legged it out to Fleatown, where Blake Richards had been living before the robbery filled his pockets.

No one had been able to tell him how much the pair took up there at Anderson's store. The only man who would have known was dead. It certainly was enough to provide a few nights of hard drinking and maybe a woman, or several.

If the amount was small, Longarm figured, the loot might already be spent and the two men broke again.

It was a funny thing, but honest folks tended to think that robbers lived high on the hog, just practically rolling in money. The truth was that the average robbery netted damned little. Longarm never heard any actual figures on the subject, but his experience after years of hunting down criminals and sitting in courtrooms afterward led him to guess the number would be less than a hundred dollars. Maybe a good deal south of the double zeroes.

And for this pittance men died.

Well, as far as he was concerned, a date with the hangman was no better than Richards and Hix deserved.

Thinking about the two—and about Harry Anderson lying dead in that hastily constructed box laid out on his own store counter—Longarm lengthened his stride.

Fleatown was just ahead.

# Chapter 41

"Di' you ever find that fella . . . I fergit what you said 'is name was. Fella running with that sonuvabitch Richards."

Longarm had to think back a while to recall the hobo he had spoken with some days earlier. Spoken with and given a dollar to, which explained why the bum remembered him and his questions.

"No. Have you seen him?" he asked.

The raggedy-assed hobo squinted and cocked his head to one side as if sizing Longarm up. "Maybe," he said.

"There's another dollar in it for you if you can tell me where he is now."

"Maybe I can. You got two dollars?"

"I offered you a dollar. Can you earn it or not? I'm not gonna stand around in this stink much longer, so if you have something to tell me, now would be the time."

The bum grumbled a little under his breath, but after a moment he said, "He come back. Yestiddy it was, I think. Him and that other fella. They was in the chips, let me tell ya. Had new blankets. Smelled like they'd had them baths. Richards, he does that sometimes when he's off to get laid. Some o' the bitches he goes with knock the price down some if a man don't smell too awful bad."

"That's interesting," Longarm said, "but where'd they go?"

"If I was gonna guess, I'd say . . . did you say you'll give me that second dollar?"

"Depends on what you have t' tell me," Longarm said.

The hobo dug a filthy fingernail into his left ear and poked around in there for a moment, then scratched in his beard. Watching him was beginning to make Longarm itch. "Place called Lady Jane's. 'Cept them ain't ladies an' her name likely ain't Jane. But if I was looking for Richards, that's where I'd start."

"All right, thanks." Longarm gave him a dollar, then turned to head back toward town, but the bum stopped him.

"Where's my other dollar?"

"Depends on what I find at this Lady Jane's."

"You won't come back here even if you do find him. You won't come back an' give me my dollar," the bum whined.

"I tell you what. You take me to Lady Jane's. If Richards is there, you'll have your dollar."

"You mean that?"

"I said it, didn't I?"

"Yeah. Awright. Lemme get my shawl. I get the miseries if I take a chill. Lemme get my shawl and I'll take you there."

The bum—he said his name was Toby, not that Longarm particularly cared—could not keep up a swift pace, so Longarm had to shorten his stride and bide his time while Toby mumbled and stumbled his way into the outskirts of Pueblo.

"Right there," he said after a ten-minute walk, pointing to a large, poorly kept up three-story house in the middle of the block. "That there is Lady Jane's. Just knock on the door."

A man wearing overalls, a knitted cap, and heavy brogans came out of the brothel. Longarm got a glimpse of a heavyset woman in the doorway behind him.

176

"That's her," Toby said. "That's Lady Jane herself."

"All right. I reckon you've earned your other dollar."

Longarm gave it to him and Toby spat out, "Richards, he's got him a new red shirt on. Or did when I seen him this morning." He bobbed his head and quickly scuttled off, likely to buy himself another bottle with his newfound wealth.

Longarm adjusted the set of his hat and walked up the short path that led from the front gate to the porch steps of the whorehouse. He rapped sharply on the door. It was opened almost immediately by the same woman he saw escorting the working-class customer out moments earlier.

"Mind another visitor, ma'am?" He removed his hat and very slightly bowed.

"Now ain't we the one with manners," Lady Jane said, fluttering her eyelashes. "Sure, come inside. Whatever you want, mister, we got it. If we don't have it, I'll find it for you." She smiled. "If you got the brass to pay for it, that is."

Longarm pushed past her into a parlor that reeked of perfume and face powder. The place was crowded, mostly with rough-dressed men who probably worked in Pueblo's mills or smelters. There were also at least eight whores in evidence, all of them on the downward side of their useful working lives. Time was already taking its toll on them. No amount of powder could cover that fact.

"Whatever you want, honey. If you don't see what you like here, I got a pair of Siamese girls upstairs. Got a girl that can suck you till your toenails curl up. Got another little gal that you'd swear wasn't a day more'n twelve if you didn't know better. And I got a real fancy one. New girl that just came to me. Oh, she's a knockout. Tall and pretty. She's picky, though. She's with a customer at the moment, but she won't be upstairs very long. I think you'll like her."

"Tell you what," Longarm said. "Let me sit down and have a drink, maybe a smoke if I can buy a cigar off you. I'll look around and make my pick when I know what I want."

177

"You just do that, sweetie. Set right down over there. Ask for whatever you want. I'll have one of my girls bring your cigar."

The madam gave him another smile and withdrew. In less than a minute, an aging whore with drooping tits and varicose veins brought him a cheap rum crook and lighted it for him. It was better than nothing. The whore, however, wouldn't have been.

He thanked her and settled back to look for Karl Hix, or for a man wearing a new red shirt.

# Chapter 42

Longarm had finished the cigar, and was thinking about asking for another to go with his second beer, when he saw a man wearing a bright red shirt. The man was fairly tall and wore his hair long and clubbed at the back of his neck. He almost had to be Blake Richards. And if Richards was in the house, likely Karl Hix was too.

Richards was on the landing at the top of the stairs. He had a redheaded floozy on one arm and a blonde on the other. He looked like a man who was enjoying himself.

Longarm set his mug aside and stood, moving to meet Richards on his way down the stairs toward the parlor below.

Shit!

Toby must have told Richards about the big man who was looking for him because the moment he laid eyes on Longarm, he stopped dead still and turned pale. His mouth worked mutely for a few seconds. Then he scowled and shoved the blond whore down the stairs while he grabbed the redhead and pulled her in front of him as a shield.

The blonde shrieked and grabbed the banister. Her feet went out from under her and she fell on her butt. She began to cry.

The redhead tried to squirm away, but Richards had her by the neck. He pulled a revolver and held it to the woman's temple.

"Get away or I'll shoot her. You know I will."

Longarm shrugged. He took his time about bringing his Colt out and pointing it up the staircase.

"I'm telling you, I'll shoot her."

"Oh, I believe you," Longarm drawled.

Behind him, there was a frenzy of shouts and thundering feet in the parlor. It was over within seconds, and the place became silent and virtually empty.

"The thing is," Longarm said in a calm and reasoning tone, "you got two choices."

Richards blinked and pushed the muzzle of his revolver harder against the side of the girl's head. Her knees sagged and she started to fall. Richards had to adjust his grip on her to keep her from dropping in front of him. She looked like she was going to pass out.

"You can shoot that girl," Longarm went on, "in which case I will shoot an' kill you. Or you can surrender to me an' take your chances with a jury o' your peers. Right now, there's one charge against you for robbing that post office. But the way I hear it, it wa'n't you as murdered Harry Anderson. Your partner done that. Right now, far as I know, there's no murder charge against you."

Of course, since a murder was committed while the robbery was taking place, Richards would be seen as equally guilty before the law and would surely hang for Anderson's murder. But Longarm saw no point in telling the man that right at this moment.

He had not lied, though. Right now there was no murder charge against Richards. That would not come until Longarm hauled him before a judge.

"Or," Longarm said, "you can go ahead an' shoot that girl. Then I'll shoot you an' we can be done with this whole thing. Now what d'you want t' do? You wanta walk away from here in manacles or d'you wanta be carried out in a pine box? Make up your mind. It don't matter none t' me."

"I think . . . I think . . . I'm scared of what happens to a fella in prison," he said.

"This ain't exactly the best time t' be thinking about that," Longarm said. "You shoulda thought o' that a long time ago." He smiled. "But let me give you a tip. If you do go t' prison, you'd best cut that long hair o' yours 'less some o' those boys decide t' turn you inta a girl."

"Oh, Jesus!" Richards moaned.

The girl he was holding lost consciousness and slipped down onto the steps below Richards.

"I didn't . . . I just . . ." Fear overcame common sense and the man's revolver turned toward Longarm.

Longarm's Colt bellowed and a pellet of hot lead smashed through the bridge of Richards's nose and battered its way through bone and brain tissue to emerge in a wet, red spray out the back of his head.

His body fell back onto the stairs, then slid down to come to rest against the whimpering, shivering redhead.

The upstairs rooms began emptying out in a stampede every bit as impassioned as the one that had cleared the parlor.

Longarm waited at the bottom of the steps while Lady Jane's patrons and her whores streamed past him. He was expecting to see Karl Hix among them, but there was no sign of the man.

One very tall and pretty whore did catch his eye. He thought she looked familiar, but he could not place where he might have seen her before. She had nice-looking legs, though. And a blond wig that was slightly askew, which was the first thing he'd noticed about her.

She brushed by him and ran straight out the front door, disappearing onto the street.

181

Longarm waited until he was sure everyone had had time to clear, even the redhead who had been upstairs with Richards; then he turned and beckoned the madam closer.

"You're a copper," she said. "I should've known. You dress too fancy for the likes of my place."

"I'm looking for the man who was with that dead one there," he said, pointing to the bloody corpse on the stairs.

"Why should I help you after all the trouble you've caused me this afternoon?"

"Maybe because you're a civic-minded person," Longarm said. "Maybe because you like t' see justice done." He smiled. "Or maybe because I'll have your place closed down till an official investigation can be completed." The smile became wider. And even less sincere. "A real long investigation."

"He's the one was with my new girl Josephine. I saw her come down. I didn't see him."

"Show me her room, would you, please."

"Since you ask so polite. Follow me."

The madam led the way to the third floor, and pointed to a door that was already standing open, probably left that way as a result of the panic when gunfire broke out. "That's Jo's room there."

Longarm palmed his Colt again and edged closer to the doorway. He peered inside.

And pushed the Colt back into its leather.

There would be no more need for shooting.

He entered the room and looked at the corpse that lay sprawled on its back on the bed.

Karl Hix was naked. Or what was left of him was.

Someone had stuffed his own socks into his mouth and worked him over with something very sharp, likely a razor. His cock and balls had been sliced off and his belly sliced open. A deep cut ran across both eyes, and his throat had been slit.

Blood soaked the bed he lay on, and a good bit of it had seeped through and was dripping onto the floor. Longarm doubted there was a spoonful left in the man's body.

Whoever did this had a real hard-on for Hix, Longarm figured. Nothing but hate could account for this.

Longarm grunted as he turned away from the sight. It looked like neither Hix nor his pal Blake Richards would be facing a jury. Well, not any jury of this world anyhow.

Longarm took his time going down the stairs. He stopped in the parlor long enough to help himself to a cigar, then went outside into the much cleaner air of crowded, smoky, fume-ridden Pueblo.

# Chapter 43

Longarm settled back onto the padded seat in one of the D&RG's newer passenger cars. He felt pretty chipper after a bath, a shave, and a good night's sleep. He felt all the better for having clean clothes, having finally recovered his missing saddle and carpetbag at the Pueblo depot.

He was thinking about walking back to the smoking car when he saw a familiar face.

"Hello, Joseph." Longarm uncrossed his legs and motioned for the handsome young man to join him.

"Just Joe now, I think. To honor my dad."

"That's a good thing for a son to do. Will you be taking the Templeton name back too? If you don't mind me asking."

"If my mother doesn't object, I will."

"Will you go back to San Francisco now?"

"Yes. It's my home. A fine city too."

Longarm looked at Joe closely. "What is it that you said you do there?"

Joe smiled. "I dance a little. Sing a little. I . . . entertain."

"You're one of those . . . what d' they call them? Female impersonators?"

Joe nodded slowly. His smile was pleasant. But unreadable.

"D'you own a razor, Joe?"

"Of course. Doesn't everyone?"

"I notice when you seen me, you didn't ask me about the hunt for the man that murdered your father."

"Didn't I?" The smile returned. "An oversight. Did you catch him?"

"I caught up with him. Someone else found him first, though."

"Really."

"He's dead."

"That's nice."

"You aren't surprised."

"Should I be?"

"No. I don't think there is any way you should be surprised by that news, Joe." Longarm stood and said, "Reckon I'll go back to the smoking car for a bit. You're welcome t' join me."

"Thank you. Perhaps later." He hesitated, then nibbled his underlip nervously for a moment. "About the person who killed Hix," he started, "are you going to . . . I mean . . ."

Longarm shook his head. "Nothing I could do about it even if I wanted to. That'd be a state offense, not federal. No, Joe, I got no interest in the woman that killed Karl Hix. Whoever she is."

Joe relaxed and smiled again, genuinely this time. "I am glad I ran into you today, Marshal."

"Yeah. Me too. Give your mom my regards, will you? She's a nice lady."

"I will do that. And . . . thank you."

Longarm turned and headed back toward the smoking car. They were approaching Fountain now. It was still a long way to Denver. And would be even farther to San Francisco.

Longarm snorted and shook his head, chuckling. Damned if Joe Templeton, Jr. didn't make a rather pretty blond woman, he thought.

Watch for

**LONGARM AND THE
HANGTREE VENGEANCE**

the 350$^{th}$ novel in the exciting LONGARM
series from Jove

*Coming in January!*

# LONGARM

## GIANT-SIZED ADVENTURE FROM AVENGING ANGEL LONGARM.

# BY TABOR EVANS

### 2006 GIANT EDITION

### LONGARM AND THE OUTLAW EMPRESS
978-0-515-14235-8

### 2007 GIANT EDITION

### LONGARM AND THE GOLDEN EAGLE SHOOT-OUT
978-0-515-14358-4